SCANDALOUS SADIE

BAD GIRLS OF THE WEST

SYLVIA MCDANIEL

VIRTUAL BOOKSELLER

Bad Girls Have More Fun

Unjustifiably branded *scandalous* by the newspaper society columnist, Sadie King tries to embrace her new identity to show society she is above such piddly gossip. She will wear her "bad girl" badge with pride, chin held high. At least until young businessman Levi Griffin decides to see just how salacious she really is.

Since rescuing a naked Sadie from a vicious prank, Levi Griffin hasn't been the same. The woman is tempting and he can't seem to walk away from her innocent smile and bewitching eyes. His mother, the local gossip writer, continuously berates the young woman, spreading lies. To top that, his mother insists that he marry the vixen who left Sadie in the dangerous situation to begin with.

For Levi, will it come down to choosing between his beloved mother who sacrificed to give him a good life and the beguiling woman he desires. Will Sadie's love for him allow such a choice or will she walk away?

CHAPTER 1

*A*ll Sadie ever wanted was to be accepted. Being the second richest young woman in town, she would've thought that wouldn't be a problem. But money didn't buy the right connections in high society or the friendships she craved—acceptance by a group of ladies in town who considered themselves society's darlings.

And yet today, she received an invitation to a picnic with none other than Nellie Robinson, the mayor's daughter. The girl who seemed to control the local young women. The one person whose words were often cutting and cruel, who decided which girls were accepted, and which ones were not. The leader of the clique.

The woman was mean if ever she had met one. Could she be ready to accept Sadie?

Preparing for the outing, Sadie, wore one of her nicest dresses with a stylish hat covering her dark hair and even an umbrella to keep the sun off her ivory complexion.

As she waited outside the house in the summer sun, she wondered if the woman would stand her up. Send her an invitation and then never arrive. It had been known to happen before.

A man in a dark suit, driving a buggy, came around the corner. The poor man must've been sweating buckets in the hot Texas heat. Nellie Robinson leaned out the window and waved to her.

"Sadie, let's go," she said.

Hurrying to the buggy, she lifted her skirts and climbed in. "Nellie, it was so kind of you to invite me."

The girl smiled. "Well, I thought it would be the perfect day for a picnic out at the springs on the other side of town. Cook prepared us a lunch. Who knows? We might even dip our toes into the water to cool off."

Sadie couldn't believe how kind Nellie was being.

"Sounds lovely and tell your cook thank you for preparing the meal," she said.

With a wave of her hand, Nellie dismissed the very thought. "That's her *job*. Daddy pays her to cook for us."

Not wanting to upset her, Sadie didn't say a word at how privileged she sounded. Her own servants were more like family.

"Are you attending the ball this weekend?"

"Yes," Sadie said, excitement rushing through her. She had a new gown she couldn't wait to wear.

Nellie's blonde hair blew in the wind as she turned her brown eyes on Sadie. "You know, Levi Griffin, the most eligible bachelor, is said to be attending. His mother, the newspaper columnist, Betty Griffin, is trying to find him a woman to marry this year. Though the man keeps insisting he's never marrying."

Sadie had seen pictures of the man. Handsome, dark hair, and emerald-green eyes, but if he didn't want to marry, why would anyone force herself on him?

"Why doesn't he want to marry?"

Nellie shrugged. "Who knows, but he is the best catch of the year, and I plan to snag him."

There wasn't a man Sadie could think of that she wanted to

snag. Was she wrong wanting them to catch her? To court her? To vie for her affections?

As the buggy rolled through the area known as Hell's Half Acre, Sadie gazed around. Her father had never approved of this part of town. He'd said it was filled with criminals and cowboys drinking and gambling. Papa was always one for propriety and she was stunned that Nellie's driver took them this way.

"Look at that saloon girl," Nellie said. "Despicable. Earning her living on her back."

An uneasy feeling skittered down Sadie's spine. Why had she wanted to be with this snobby young woman? She didn't like Nellie and yet here they were on their way out of town to the springs. She changed the subject. "Did you purchase a new gown for the ball?" she asked her hostess.

The girl smiled. "It's exquisite. Mother had the dressmaker get the latest patterns from New York. It will be beautiful and I'll be the prettiest girl at the ball."

Sadie gave her a weak smile. "I'm sure you will be."

"Oh, look here is the springs. I love this place."

This pond, with a small waterfall from a river that fed the lake, had lush vegetation and big oak trees. A natural spring, the water was clear and cool.

The driver pulled the buggy to a halt, set the brake, and stepped down to help them alight. The place was deserted and an eerie feeling skirted up Sadie's spine. Almost a warning.

"Robert, place our picnic on the ground and then do not be within sight for a while."

He spread a blanket out and then set a basket down. "Yes, ma'am. Anything else?"

"Just wait on the road. I'll call you when I'm ready to go."

"Yes, ma'am," he said and crawled into the wagon and drove off, leaving them alone.

They both sat on the blanket, then Nellie opened the basket, and fixed a plate. She handed it to Sadie. "Bon appétit."

After Sadie had taken a few bites of the food, she smiled. "Delicious," she said. "I'm so glad we're doing this."

An impertinent smile crossed the young woman's face. Since their days in school, this was the friendliest Nellie had ever been to Sadie. Maybe the young woman had changed.

"You've been alone since your papa died?" Nellie asked.

"Yes, my servants have been with me for years, so they protect me."

"You can do whatever you want."

"Not really. My maid watches over me very carefully."

"That's not the same," Nellie said. "You're free."

What she meant by free, Sadie didn't have a clue, but she wasn't about to argue with the woman.

They finished the meal and then Nellie turned to her with a wicked smile. "Let's go swimming."

"What? Ladies don't swim," Sadie said.

Nellie stood and began to remove her clothes. "This lady does. Come, no one is here. No one will see us. We can cool off in the water."

The thought of cooling off sounded wonderful. It was a hot summer day, and Sadie did want to belong to Nellie's group of friends.

"All right," she said as Nellie ran stark naked into the clear, sparkling spring water.

Glancing around, Sadie hung her clothes on a bush and then ran as fast as her long legs would carry her into the water. The cool wash was like a breath of fresh air. Nellie was swimming out to the center of the pool and Sadie reluctantly followed her. She was a weak swimmer at best.

When they reached the middle, Nellie grinned at her. "Isn't this refreshing?"

"Yes," Sadie admitted.

Nellie went even farther out and Sadie followed, wondering how far she intended to go.

When they were near the small waterfall, she laughed gleefully. "Race you to the bank."

She took off and Sadie knew she would never catch her. When she reached the bank, Nellie grinned at her.

"Not much of a swimmer, are you?"

"Not really," she said.

"Race you to the falls again," she said, taking off splashing her arms. By this time, Sadie was winded and arrived a lot later than Nellie.

They paddled about in the water and then Nellie glanced at her. "I never really thought you would come out here with me."

How did she respond without sounding desperate?

"I've wanted to be your friend for quite some time," Sadie told her. "You've never shown any interest in being sociable with me. And I thought this would be a good chance to get to know you."

The girl smiled. "My daddy is the richest man in town. I'm very careful about who I choose to be my friends."

Sadie nodded. She could see that.

"Even though your father left you a lot of money, you're kind of an oddball. An outcast, even though you're quite beautiful."

"Thank you," Sadie said, hoping she meant that as a compliment.

"But we'll never be friends. In fact, you're going to hate me," she said with a wicked grin.

A trickle of alarm spiraled through Sadie as she wondered at her statement. What did she mean, hate her?

"Last one back remains behind," she said and took off toward the shore.

Stunned, Sadie glanced at her. *Last one back...behind?*

Dear God, no!

Immediately, she swam as fast as she could. By the time she reached the shore, Nellie had grabbed *all* the clothes, the picnic items, and was making a naked dash to the buggy.

When she reached the waiting vehicle, she shouted to her

driver. "Let's go." The man stared at her nude form as she screamed at him. "I said let's go."

"What about the other young woman?"

"We're leaving her behind."

The man shook his head and climbed into the buggy. At the shore, Sadie stood and watched as her nemesis drove off, taking with her every stitch of clothing she'd been tricked into doffing.

Dear God, what did she do now?

CHAPTER 2

*L*evi Griffin drove his buggy toward Fort Worth, ready to reach home. He'd spent most of the day in Dallas discussing a property he was considering to build his next hotel on. But something about the land, the price, and the location of being not far from the Trinity River, left him with doubts.

The sun was setting and he shielded his eyes from the bright orange glow that ruminated from the west. His horse knew the way and the buggy meandered along the trail.

"Sir," he heard a voice yell.

Surprised, he glanced around seeing no one. "I must be hearing things."

"Sir," a female screamed, "please stop."

He pulled the wagon to a halt, letting his eyes search the heavily wooded area alongside the road. There was nobody there. Finally, he noticed rustling in the bushes and then the most beautiful creature stepped out from behind a cedar shrub.

She had taken branches and placed them in specific areas of her naked body, hiding as much as possible from his view.

And it was still quite a sight. The woman had long legs and a slender waist and her breasts were hidden from his eyes. Her long dark hair was half pinned up and the other half falling around her face that framed large sapphire eyes, the color of Texas bluebonnets in spring. His eyes drank in her straight nose, high cheekbones, and full lips that were ripe for kissing.

But what was she doing out here naked?

"I need your help," she said, her bottom lip trembling. Her eyes filled with tears.

How long had she been here? Was this a trap? He glanced around looking for thieves to jump out.

"What happened? Are you all right?"

"I'm fine," she said. "Someone pulled a mean prank on me."

"I'd say," he said, stepping down from his buggy cautious not to approach her too quickly. Still watching the surrounding area carefully.

"You've not been…" How did he say the unthinkable?

"No," she said, taking a step back. Not really wanting him to come too close.

She was vulnerable, so beautiful, and such easy prey out here.

"Your clothes are gone?"

"Yes, she took them with her," she said in a huff.

He wanted to ask who would do such a thing but would not pry. If she wanted to tell him, he would listen.

"Do you have a blanket?" she asked.

"Sorry, I only carry one in the buggy during the winter." He started to unbutton his cuffs. "Here, wear my shirt."

"Thank you," she said, timidly reaching out to take the garment.

She stepped behind the bush and he could hear her slipping on his offered clothing. How in the world could he ever wear that shirt again without thinking of her? Even now, the thought of her full breasts beneath the soft material was enough to make him sigh.

The woman was beautiful. Her face was a touch pinkish, but

that was probably from being out in the sun too long. The long dark lashes that framed her eyes made his heart beat a little faster.

He had to know her name.

When she stepped out from behind the brush, her cheeks were even more pink, and she tugged and pulled on the shirt, trying to make it as long as possible. It fell right below her womanly parts and he knew that if the wind blew, he would see everything.

Her breasts filled out the top portion nicely and he could tell she was mortified.

"I'm Levi Griffin, by the way."

"Sadie King," she said.

"Your father was Edward King who sold a lot of cattle," he said with a grin.

"Yes," she said. "Do you know where I live?"

"Silk Stocking Bluffs?" he said.

"Yes," she said. "Is your mother Betty Griffin, the social columnist in the paper?"

Already he could see her worry and understood her reasoning. His mother was the most spiteful, vindictive woman for the newspaper and the sweet motherly type at home. It was like living with two different women.

The dual personalities didn't mesh well. Sometimes, he accused her of being soundly mad, but she was his mother and he was her only son.

"Yes, she is. But I think this little outing will be just between the two of us," he said, trying to reassure the woman. If his mother learned about what happened to this young woman, she would exploit it and ruin the woman's reputation.

"Shall we get you home before the mosquitos make a feast off you?" He offered her his hand to help her into the buggy.

"Thank you," she said, tugging the shirt down.

He tried not to look, he really did, but there was her beautiful firm back end that connected to long legs.

All he could think about was the way those limbs would feel wrapped around his waist as he plunged his cock into her.

But that was a thought he shoved aside. The poor woman needed his help.

"We'll go the backroads toward your home. That way, maybe no one will see us, each half undressed," he said, knowing the odds of that were zero to none, but he wanted to try for her sake. "Was this done intentionally?"

"Oh, yes," she said. "I've been naive far too long. The person who did this will have the favor returned to her. Especially if she ruins me. And that's what she was trying to do. I have no doubt."

As he climbed up into the buggy, he nodded and glanced at her. "Women can be vicious."

She laughed and he was so glad he put a smile on her face. "Yes, they can be. But men have their quirks as well."

"What? How can that be?" he said with a smile as he clucked to the horses and slapped the reins. He wanted to remove the sadness from her eyes and make her smile once again. The wagon began to roll and she glanced back at the springs.

"I've always loved this spot and she ruined it for me."

"No, don't let her ruin your previous experiences there. If possible, forget what happened to you today. All that you've suffered is a little embarrassment and humiliation." It was true, though he would love to see her all dressed up. The woman would be a stunner.

"We'll try to get you home without being ruined," he said, thinking if anyone found out, they could blame him. After all, the woman was nude beneath his shirt.

She sighed. "Do you know how much pressure there is on a woman to find the perfect match? Not to do anything that might hurt her reputation or sully her good name. And yet, there are women out there who would like nothing more than to get rid of their competition."

"Oh, I know about the pressure of finding a bride," he said. "I'm supposed to be the catch of the season."

Her mouth dropped open and she turned and stared at him. Her sapphire eyes wide and twinkling with laughter. "Oh my goodness, yes. I was told that today."

"So, see? I have just as many people scrutinizing me."

She started to laugh outrageously. Her hand covered her mouth as she giggled and he wondered at the joke.

"What is so funny?" he said, smiling at her. Why he felt at ease with her, he didn't know. But there was an easiness between them, even with her nude body so close to his.

"The girl who did this to me, she thinks you are perfect for her. She's coming after you. I'd run far away if I were you." His brows rose as he stared at the woman laughing. "The irony of this situation is she placed me in a terrible position, and who did I meet? None other than the man she is going to pursue. And I met him first because of her mean prank."

"Would you like to tell me who this woman is?"

Sadie laughed even harder. "Oh no. I want to see if you figure out who is intent on catching you at this year's balls."

With a sigh, he glanced at her and smiled. "I would not even attend those stuffy affairs, but for my mother. She insists and then she pushes the most awful women toward me. Does your mother do that to you?"

A dark cloud crossed her face. "My mother died in childbirth and, as you know, my father has been dead for several years. I'm alone."

"I'm so sorry," he said, wishing he could put the smile back on her face. "All right, you're not going to tell me. But if I should guess after the first ball, will you agree to have dinner with me?"

She gave him a saucy grin that made his insides heat. Even

though this situation was perilous, they were laughing at the absurdity of it.

"We'll see," she said. "You get me home without me losing my reputation, then dinner is my treat."

"No," he said, "a woman doesn't buy my dinner."

"Fine, we'll put it on my father's tab and he'll pay for dinner."

"But he's dead."

"He still has a tab at the Cattleman's Steak House," she said.

Cowboys on horseback rode not far from them as they drew closer to the city. As much as he was enjoying this conversation, it was time to get her home before dark.

"A dead man with a tab. Interesting," he said.

"It's for his family whenever we go. We're always treated with the utmost respect. Father used to make sure they received the best beef. Without him, the eatery may not have made it in the early years, so he told me."

Several minutes later, they turned down the street. The mansions before him were gorgeous as they faced west with the setting sun.

"Which house is yours?" A sinking feeling overcame him as he saw a crowd of people standing in front of one house. A reporter with one of those new flash picture boxes stood waiting.

"Oh no," he said, his heart dropping like a rock. They knew and lay in wait for her.

She sat up and shook her head. "Why did I think she would play fair? She alerted the newspaper that I would be coming home without my clothes."

Whoever this woman was, she was ruthless, and he wanted nothing to do with her.

"Is there a way around the back?"

"No. I'm ruined," she said with a sigh.

"Don't give up yet," he said and turned the horses around.

"Where are you going?" she asked, her blue eyes growing large.

"There must be another way for you not to be seen," he said.

He drove the team around the block and just when he thought they were going to escape, they ran into the crowd surging toward them.

"Miss King, where are your clothes?" a reporter called.

"No questions," Levi announced with command. They were blocked in, the buggy surrounded with people waiting to ask her questions.

He turned and stared at her. "I'll come around to your side and we'll make a dash to your front door. Let me wrap my arms around you to protect you. Also to keep them from taking pictures."

She sighed and shook her head. "That strumpet is going to learn about revenge."

Levi hopped out of the buggy and raced to the other side. He helped her alight. But instead of letting him cover her, she walked like a queen up the sidewalk to the front door with him trailing.

His shirt hung barely to her thighs as she walked barefoot up to the door, ignoring anyone who tried to speak to her. All she needed was a crown on her head.

When they reached the entrance, she turned to him. "Thank you for rescuing me today. I appreciate it. I'll get the shirt back to you."

A smile crossed Levi's face. "Keep the shirt. All I would do is think of you, if you brought it back."

She grinned. "Good evening, Levi."

"Let's do this again," he said.

She smiled and then walked inside the house, shutting the door and all of them out.

CHAPTER 3

*T*he next morning, Levi sat at his table in his private
hotel room reading the newspaper and drinking
coffee. His maid, Lily, refilled his cup as he read his mother's
latest installment in her gossip column.

Dear Readers,

*The most scandalous event happened yesterday in our growing cow
town. Just when you think the streets are becoming less crime filled, a
daring young miss was seen riding in a carriage wearing nothing more
than a man's shirt. Sadie King, daughter of our own Edward King, rode
naked through town with a young man who was shirtless himself!*

*Seems she'd gone skinny dipping at the springs and somehow her
horse must have gotten away along with her clothes. If not for the good
citizen (or was he?) who picked her up and brought her home, she would
have had to walk through town naked.*

*A young woman should always be protective of her reputation. Now
her innocence has been ruined and who is going to want to marry this
little hussy?*

*With the first ball happening this weekend, I've decided that I shall
now call her Scandalous Sadie.*

Toodles,

Betty Griffin
Look to this space for more juicy gossip.

Rage consumed him and he slammed his coffee cup on the table, causing it to slosh out of the cup.

"Damn it, Mother," he yelled, standing from his chair. He stormed out the door and went down the hotel main stairs two flights and stopped at his mother's door.

He banged on the door and her servant opened it. "Yes, Mr. Griffin."

He walked past her not responding to her question. "Mother. Mother, where are you?"

His gray-haired, innocent-looking mother, hurried from the small kitchenette where she was having her coffee and toast. Still in her robe, she gazed at him like he was a boy of ten instead of mid-twenties.

"Whatever are you yelling for, Levi? What's wrong?"

"Your damn gossip column is what's wrong. You don't have all the facts," he said, wondering how she got away with such slanderous lies.

"And I suppose you do?"

"Yes, I have most of them. You must know that *I* was the citizen who picked her up. Who rescued her. She was kind enough not to say who had done this to her. Why didn't you come speak to me before you printed this rubbish or is it only lies you wish to publish?"

She smiled at him in that way that he deplored. It was a smirk that said *I'm right and you're wrong. And nothing you can say will make me change my opinion.*

"I rescued her yesterday. This woman was left stranded without her clothes as some kind of practical joke. The woman who did it knew it would ruin her if she were caught. And when I pulled up in front of her home, there were the reporters waiting. She didn't have a chance. The vicious woman who did this was serious about making certain she was caught."

Walking back into the kitchenette area, she sank into her chair and took a sip of her coffee. Then she glanced at him over her cup. "What can I say? She should have known better than to go skinny dipping. She is supposed to be a high-class lady in our cow town where we are trying to make society work. It was wrong and she was caught."

"More like set up," he said.

"Do you think I care that some other girl was smart enough to oust her competition?"

This was what he hated about his mother. Her rules of comportment were so outdated that he wanted to scream every time he read her column. Especially when he knew what she said was a lie.

Someday, it would come back and hurt her. Someday, someone was going to get tired of half-truths and seek retaliation.

"So you would let this girl be banished from society because she was fooled by a girl with no morals?" he said, gazing at the woman who had raised him alone. He didn't remember his father at all.

As long as he could recall, it had just been the two of them.

She smiled. "Someday when you have children, you'll understand. You want the very best for your children and this kind of behavior is *not* what I'm looking for in a wife for you."

"Who said she would be considered as a wife for me?"

"Like I said, we're finding you a wife this year. It's time. When you have children, you'll understand the need to protect them from unscrupulous women."

Oh, dear God, Lecture Number 125 about "you'll understand someday." Hell, he was twenty-six years old. How much longer did he have to wait until the wand of understanding descended upon him?

"So, you like the person who tricked her better because she was mean enough to trap her competition."

His mother smiled. "Now you understand, son. A mother wants the best for her children. Smart, driven, and above reproach. I want your wife to be the best society has to offer."

Stunned, he shook his head. The woman delighted in gossip and yet he loved her with all his heart. But he hated that damn column she wrote that made her sound so pompous while she lived in *his* hotel. She resided here and paid no rent.

With a sigh, he shook his head.

"Do you have your suits all clean and pressed?"

"Yes," he said, thinking he was no longer irresponsible. He knew how to dress and take care of himself.

"Good, did you get your shirt back from that hussy?"

"No, I told her to keep it," he said, thinking how he could never wear that garment again without thinking of and smelling her scent. "You know, Mother, she was really a beautiful woman. And I liked how she handled this prank. She didn't tell me the name of the girl who did this to her. She didn't go into hysterics but remained calm and in control."

Pursing her lips, she shook her head. "Not a smart move. She should have started a war by telling who did this to her and then we could have sat back and watched to see who ruined the other first."

That was it. He had to get out of here. He needed to get away before he exploded. Before he said things he would later regret.

"By the way, I'm making a list of girls for you to dance with at the ball. These girls are very high society with spotless reputations. Any would make an excellent wife."

Great, she was still on a "find his bride" crusade. Even suggesting women for him to court. Right now, he felt too much pressure to choose a woman from her list, and so therefore, none of them would he even consider.

"Promise me you will at least dance with them," she said.

"Absolutely, Mother, and then I'll bring them to you for inspection," he said, being sarcastic.

"That's not a bad idea, son," she said. "That way I can approve."

His mouth dropped open and he spun on his heel and walked out of the room. She didn't even realize he was mocking her. What she didn't know was that he had no plans on getting married this year.

Just like Sadie, he was not going to settle for someone he didn't want and he was tired of being pressured.

At this point, he would show up at the ball to make an appearance and then he would be gone. He would spend the rest of the night maybe gambling or drinking with his friends. Anything to upset his mother.

CHAPTER 4

*S*adie was nervous. Her new ball gown was gorgeous with white satin tulle and lace, the back dipping precariously. The color made her dark hair and lashes seem even darker.

As they pulled up in front of one of the new mansions, she waited for her driver to open the door of the carriage. This was the first ball of the newly formed season. For the last three years, the women of Fort Worth had arranged summertime balls trying to mimic those held in New York.

In some ways, it was kind of funny, but Sadie did enjoy attending. She only wished her father was still here with her. If he were, he would scoff at the article in the paper and tell her to get in there and have a good time.

He would wander over to speak to the men and drink a whiskey, but he was gone. And she was now alone.

The door opened and her driver held out his hand. "Miss, you look stunning tonight."

"Thank you, Cletus. I'll send word to you when I'm ready to leave," she said.

"Yes, ma'am," he said with a nod.

The men and women who worked for her, she deeply respected, and they felt more like family than servants. Most of them had been with the family since she was a child.

She strung her small reticule around her wrist. Inside, she carried a small pair of scissors, a needle and thread, and a little pot of lip coloring.

After she climbed the steps to the mansion doors, she lifted the silk skirt of her dress and entered the ballroom. This was the second year she had attended alone and it was always nerve wracking to go by herself. She missed her dad's presence at times like this.

Helen Davis, one of the mean girls, stood just inside the doorway. Her mouth dropped open and brows rose when she saw Sadie. Sadie walked past and smiled.

"Good evening, Helen. Your dress looks lovely."

The woman didn't respond, but immediately turned her back on her. With a sigh, Sadie continued into the ballroom. So she was to be shunned this evening all because of Nellie.

Seth Robinson, Nellie's brother, gave her a wicked grin like he was imagining her naked. The man was a sharpshooter with a rifle, but she considered him a whining momma's boy. Quickly she went in another direction looking for her friend Rose Tuttle.

Rose stood talking with a sibling in the corner. Sadie waved at her and her friend frowned. Then she separated herself from her sister and hurried over to Sadie.

"What are you doing here?"

Sadie frowned. "Why wouldn't I be here?"

"The paper," Rose said. "You, my dear friend, are no longer part of society. You are to be hung at noon for not remaining the pure, innocent, lady not tainted by scandal."

"Why? Because Nellie left me at the lake after tricking me into taking my clothes off? Nothing happened except a nice young man saved me."

She shook her head and shivered at the thought of what could have happened that day. "Funny thing, the man who rescued me is the very reason all that happened. Nellie wanted to make certain I didn't go after her man, the catch of the season, Levi Griffin."

Rose started to laugh. "Like his mother would let you anywhere near her precious son."

The music began to play and men and women were on the dance floor. Rose and Sadie stepped away.

"Where's Nellie?" Sadie asked.

"Don't look, but she's dancing with your rescuer," Rose said.

Sadie smiled. "I'm not surprised. And if he makes her happy, I hope she catches him."

Though a part of her knew that statement was not true. There was something about Levi that made her smile. The man had tried his best to put her at ease, even when he walked her almost naked through a throng of reporters to her front door.

Levi and Nellie whirled past them on the dance floor and Levi nodded at her.

"So just because that mean girl tricked me, I'm no longer welcome to attend society events?"

"Sweetie, my father warned me from speaking to you tonight," Rose said.

Rose's father was the famous preacher Reverend Tuttle at the First Baptist Church of Fort Worth – the largest congregation in the city. And he had been on a campaign to clean up Fort Worth. To rid the streets of the drunken cowboys, the cribs where the prostitutes lived, and to get rid of the gambling halls.

So far, the city was trying to clean up, but the wild streets of the Acre were still going strong.

"Rose," a deep voice called, her father giving her the parental evil eye that she was disobeying.

She sighed. "Speak of the devil. The man will not let me live my life."

"Rose, get over here," he said, loud enough that people were turning to stare.

"Go, it's all right. I'll talk to you soon."

The preacher's daughter could not be seen with the latest scandalous woman. Sadie was tempted to attend his church tomorrow, but that would just cause trouble.

"Be careful," Rose warned her.

She leaned against the column like a wallflower, waiting for any man to ask her to dance, anyone to speak to her, but everyone walked a wide path around her. She felt more alone than ever before.

Nellie's evil prank had certainly made her an outcast.

"Miss King," a deep voice said, "I didn't recognize you with your clothes on."

Shaking her head, she smiled at him and stared into the most mischievous pair of emerald eyes she'd ever met. A thrill of antic-ipation spiraled through her. "Are you sure you want to be seen talking to me? It seems I must have typhoid or yellow fever tonight."

"Not only do I want to speak to you, I'd like to dance with you," Levi said.

"Oh, you really do want to get a black mark on your reputa-tion," she said. "You see that corner of society mothers? They're not going to let you dance with their daughters."

He leaned down toward her ear. "I don't care. Now, will you dance with me?"

Sadie thought about it for a second and then grinned. Why not? What did she have to lose?

She put her hand in his. "With pleasure."

He whirled her out on the dance floor and they moved in unison like they had been dancing together for years.

"You're a very good dancer," he whispered against her ear.

"And so are you," she responded, gazing into his eyes. "I still owe you that dinner for rescuing me."

"Anytime you're available," he said.

They waltzed past his mother, and Sadie noted the rigid set of her face as she watched her son.

"I get the feeling your mother is not happy about you dancing with me."

"No, she gave me a list of the appropriate women to dance with tonight and your name was not on the list. And, frankly, I'm not dancing with the women on the list unless you tell me which one is out to pursue me."

What did she say? He had already danced with Nellie and now he was dancing with her, which would make Nellie furious.

"No, I'm waiting to see if you figure her out."

His brows drew together in a frown. "Is she here tonight?"

"Oh, yes," she said laughing. "Right now, she's probably shooting daggers at my back."

"Then we shall dance again later tonight, so you can continue to rile her. After all, she did you a great injustice."

The song was coming to an end and he escorted her back to where she had been standing alone.

People stared at them, and she leaned closer to him, giving the crowd even more reason to watch.

"Mr. Griffin, thank you," she said.

"You're welcome, Miss King. We'll dance again later," he said, and with a quick bow, he walked away.

While many of the men here were married, there were a few single ones standing around watching. With a sigh, she decided to go into the ladies' room.

No sooner had she stepped inside than in followed Nellie.

"Why are you here? Do you not realize you have been disgraced? You need to leave now."

Sadie turned and smiled at her nemesis. "Hello, Nellie. Your dress is beautiful." While Sadie wanted to scratch her eyes out, she was slowly reeling her in like a bass caught in the river.

The woman stopped and stared at her in surprise. "That's not going to work."

"What? It's true."

"Why are you here? Don't you have any dignity? You're not wanted here."

"Do you wish that I go to Mrs. Griffin and tell her what truly happened?"

Her nemesis' eyes grew large and the color drained from her face. "You wouldn't."

"Why not? That way she would have the real story," Sadie said, wishing Nellie would turn around and walk out the door.

"What you did to me was dangerous. What if I had been raped? Did you think of the harm that could have befallen me?"

The girl frowned. "No, and I really didn't care."

Sadie wanted to rip her hair out, strand by strand, but that would only be a temporary satisfaction.

"By the way, guess who happened to pass by when I was in such dire straits?" Sadie could not contain the smile that spread across her face. Nellie was not going to like this answer.

She licked her lips nervously, her brows drawn together. "Who?"

"Levi Griffin. He was such a gentleman. He gave me his shirt to wear and even drove me home."

"No, he did not," she said, her eyes widening with what looked like hate. Her body stiffened and it was all Sadie could do to keep from laughing.

"So, you see, by doing to me what you did, you introduced me to your intended. I told him there was a woman here who was determined to catch him."

"You did not," she said, her face going pale.

"Oh, yes, but I didn't give him your name. He's trying to learn from me who, but it's more of game between us. You know, he's a very nice man."

The woman's fists clenched and she all but stomped her foot.

"Damn you, Sadie, I wanted you gone. Your reputation is ruined."

"Thank you for doing that. Now I know who my real friends are and it's really opened my eyes to how *bad* girls probably never meant to get into trouble. Who knows? I'm thinking about creating a bad girls' club. A place where we can all gather and talk about who ruined us."

The woman's eyes widened again. "You wouldn't dare."

"Oh, yes, I would," Sadie said softly.

Nellie shook her head. "Please don't tell Levi it's me. Please don't tell him what I did to you."

Sadie reached out and squeezed her hand in a comforting manner. She had to build her trust if she was going to do what she had planned.

"Why would I? This way we're closer. Because you know the first time you do anything else to me, I'm going to tell the man you want to marry who is pursuing him. And he will think you are a wanton gold digger only interested in what he can give you."

The woman bit her lip and sighed. "Let's just keep this between the two of us."

"For now," Sadie said with a smile.

"I'm going back out," Nellie said. "I'm trusting you to keep your promise."

Sadie smiled. "Oh, I will."

Nellie whirled around and just as she reached the door, Sadie called out.

"Oh no," Sadie said. "You have a small tear in your dress."

"What? You're lying," Nellie said.

"No, I'm being honest with you," Sadie said. "Wait, I have a needle and thread in my reticule."

She pulled Nellie closer to the lamp. "Right here," she said, pushing her finger into the seam creating a hole.

"Let me get my sewing kit out." Quietly as possible, she took the scissors out and slowly she began to cut a hole the size of the woman's ass in her dress. "A couple more stitches and no one will ever know." She tugged and jostled the dress.

"Did you fix it?"

"Oh, yes, I did," Sadie said. "You're as good as new."

With a sigh, the woman headed out the door. Not even a thank you, but then again, Sadie didn't care.

With a giggle, she followed Nellie out the door. Let the fun begin. Mrs. Griffin stood waiting for her.

"You need to leave," she said.

"Why?"

"Because you are not a reputable young woman. I've spoken to your driver and he's waiting outside for you."

Sadie had had enough. Besides, the eruption would soon happen when Nellie realized she'd been had. That her ass was showing to the members of society.

"I'm going to leave, but not because of you, Mrs. Griffin. I wonder if you have ever been deceived like I was. I wonder if anyone has ever hurt and disappointed you. Maybe you should try writing something nice in your columns, instead of the evil you spout."

Sadie didn't know where that came from, but it felt good to tell the woman off.

"Leave now," the woman commanded.

"Have a wonderful evening," Sadie said as she walked toward the door.

The silly woman followed her at a distance. Tears filled Sadie's eyes, but she would not let anyone see her cry.

Suddenly a scream came from across the room and she smiled. "Sounds like someone's derriere is hanging out," she said as she walked out the front door, the night air greeting her.

Mrs. Griffin stopped in the doorway, and it was then that Sadie saw Levi standing outside talking to Hayden Lee, a wealthy railroad owner.

A wicked idea came to her as she walked to the man she admired. She stopped, smiled at him, and then pulled his chin down to her level, where her lips met his and she kissed him.

In some ways, it was awkward since she'd never kissed anyone before. But a thrill spiraled through her when he took over the kiss, his lips moving over hers, returning the kiss.

"Levi," his mother cried out in a voice a mother would use for a seven-year-old.

Sadie broke the kiss and grinned up at him. "Good night, Levi. I've been dismissed."

With that, she turned and walked away. As much as she enjoyed the kiss, she also felt hurt. She was not going to accept that she'd been ruined.

All because she'd trusted one of the mean girls.

CHAPTER 5

*A*ll night, Levi had dreamed of that kiss. The sauciness of her walking out the door and grabbing his chin and kissing him. In front of his mother!

She kissed like an innocent. Like someone who had never kissed before, but she did it in a way that seized his attention.

Shortly after her attention grabbing departure, he walked back into the ballroom to tell his mother he was leaving when there was quite a commotion. It seemed that Nellie Robinson's dress had suffered a terrible accident. The entire seat of her dress was cut, exposing her pantaloons.

The woman was in hysterics that everyone had seen her undergarments as she twirled on the dance floor. And she kept screaming, "I'll get even with that wench."

A smile crept across his face and he knew Sadie had gotten her revenge. It was Nellie who left her out at the springs on the far side of Fort Worth. Nellie wanted to pursue him, and yet, she was the woman he liked the least.

No matter what, he wasn't interested in getting married. Every year, his mother pushed harder and harder, and he resisted more and more. When the right woman came along, he'd succumb, but for now, he liked his life. And he refused to let his mother decide who he should marry.

As he sat in his kitchen gazing out at the streets of Fort Worth, a knock sounded on his door.

His housekeeper opened the door and his mother stormed in. "What a disaster. That Sadie King ruined last night's ball."

"Really?" This was news? It seemed to him that most of the people there had shunned her all because of his mother. And that angered him, but he didn't know how to stop her. If he said anything to his mother, she would only make it worse for Sadie.

"And I couldn't believe you let that hussy kiss you. Please tell me you were just pacifying her. The girl is nothing but trouble."

"The kiss was quite delightful," he said, knowing his statement would irritate his mother.

"Levi," she said in shock.

"It's the truth," he said. "I hope I get a chance to kiss her again."

That kiss he'd relived over and over last night, and if he got an opportunity, he was determined he would show the delightful Miss King exactly how a kiss was supposed to happen. Hers wasn't bad, but he could make it so much better.

His kiss would leave her knees weak and heart pounding. And that's how he liked to kiss a woman.

"That despicable woman ruined Nellie Robinson's beautiful dress and exposed her to everyone on the dance floor. The poor girl was beside herself. I thought maybe today you could go by and take her flowers. Try to cheer her up after her embarrassing ordeal."

Right here and now, he needed to let his mother know how he felt about Nellie.

"That is not going to ever happen," he said and took a sip of his coffee, waiting for the explosion.

It didn't take long.

"That girl needs someone to console her. It's the least you can do," she said, taking a seat at his breakfast table like she had planted herself and intended to stay.

"And taking her flowers and trying to cheer her up would look like I was trying to court her, and it will be a cold day in hell before I would ever consider that immature woman."

His mother's mouth dropped and her face crumpled like she couldn't believe he would say this.

"Why not? She's the best woman available this year. You could not do any better. Her father is the mayor. And they have wealth and power."

Maybe his mother considered her the best of the eligible young woman, but Levi knew better. He saw through Nellie's cunning scheme. The woman was overly dramatic, created drama, and was a royal she-devil to other people. He'd seen her in action. Not wife material. He also knew that his mother was only concerned about their place in society, which he couldn't care less about.

"If I wanted to live with a shrew, she would be the perfect candidate. No, Mother, and do not press me any further on this."

His mother narrowed her eyes at him. "Is this what Sadie told you about her?"

He laughed. His mother just wouldn't give up and she was determined to say the rudest things about Sadie. Maybe that was why he was enjoying the woman, but he didn't think so. There was something about the way she smiled and those bedazzling eyes. One glance and he wanted to sweep her off her feet and kiss her senseless.

"No. Sadie did not say anything bad about any of the women, even though someone left her naked at the springs. I have my suspicions as to whom, especially since Miss Robinson's dress was damaged last night."

A smile crossed his mother's face. "Frankly, if Nellie did that to Sadie, I think it was rather smart of her."

"And I think it was cruel. Ruthless and without heart."

"Well, what do you think of what Sadie did to Nellie's dress?"

He thought for a moment. "She could have done much worse to the girl. I would have stripped her naked and pushed her out the door."

She sighed. "You really don't like Nellie?"

"Not at all. There was no connection between us. Nothing. I couldn't wait to get off the dance floor with her."

"What about Helen Davis or Carrie Miller?"

She picked up a leftover biscuit and buttered it, like she was trying to butter him up. She lost on the first pick, now she was moving on to girl number two and three.

This would get her goat. After dancing with Sadie, he hadn't been interested in any of the other women. In fact, he left not long after Sadie.

"I didn't dance with them," he said.

"I gave you a list," she said, her eyes flashing with annoyance.

"And I've told you that I'm not getting married. You're wasting your time and building up hopes with these girls. There will be no marriage in my immediate future." *If ever.*

And maybe his stubbornness was a little way of getting back at his mother for writing such a horrific article about Sadie. But none of these girls interested him at all.

"You're the most eligible bachelor this year. You're the one everyone is hoping to catch."

"Good luck to them. I'm also the one who doesn't want to get caught. So don't be planning a wedding."

His mother rose from the table and walked to the coffee bar and poured herself a drink. "Why are you being such an obstinate son? Why don't you want to marry? There will be the marriage bed, children, heirs to your fortune."

With a sigh, he shook his head. "Right now, my business takes my time. I'm enjoying being a single man. I'm in no hurry. And I don't like the women you're throwing at me. I don't like you trying to choose who I'm going to marry."

He picked up his coffee cup and downed the rest of the warm liquid.

"Now, Mother, if you'll excuse me. They are expecting me at the bank to discuss buying land," he said, setting his coffee cup down and standing.

Land he hoped to build a hospital on if approved by the city. A project that was near and dear to his heart. A project that he hoped the citizens of Fort Worth would appreciate.

A last glance at his mother showed her frowning at him. The woman just refused to give up on finding him a wife. Was it wrong of him to want to locate the woman himself? Who he wanted to be the mother of his children?

As much as he loved his mother, she could be trying to say the least.

CHAPTER 6

*A*fter the disastrous ball, Sadie decided to hold her own ball. Hurriedly, she made plans, sent out the invitations and the servants prepared food. Two weeks from now, she expected to hold a grand event with a buffet, a band, and even a singer.

She couldn't wait to show up Nellie Robinson.

For once, she would outshine the callous girl and show her up.

Rose was going to sing which would get her back into the good graces of society, she just knew it. Because everyone certainly loved a party and Sadie had held grand events before.

The day came and all the food was ready, the band was warming up, and her servants were ready to assist the partygoers.

Ten minutes after eight, no one had arrived, including Rose. At ten minutes to nine, the door opened and in stepped Levi.

For a moment, her heart skipped a beat at the sight of him. Tall and handsome, his green eyes sparkled with mischief. While she was so happy to see him, she also felt humiliated. No one else had attended. They all shunned her once again.

"Good evening, Miss King," he said, smiling at her.

"Good evening, Levi," she said. "It was nice of you to come. As you can see, you're the only one here. Not even my good friend Rose or Nellie have shown up."

He nodded sympathetically.

"That's because your nemesis, Nellie Robinson is holding a grand ball at the Mayor's Mansion."

"But nothing was planned," Sadie said, thinking once again Nellie managed to outdo her.

"It was thrown together at the last minute."

"Of course, it was." She couldn't help but roll her eyes.

"Rose is there with her father, and you know how the man likes to bind his daughter to his side whenever he thinks she's going to rebel."

It was odd that he'd noticed this. Rose and she spoke of it often and it frustrated her friend to no end. "Did you see Tessa?"

"No. I'm sure she's out shooting targets somewhere and forgot all about attending your ball."

"She's preparing for the National Rifleman's Competition." Sadie waved her hand, brushing away Tessa's absence. "Nellie got me again." This explained a lot. The reason why no one was here.

"How did you figure out she was my nemesis? The one who left me at the springs?"

He laughed. "Oh, that was easy. Who else would have cut her dress? After you left, I walked into the ballroom with a woman in full blown hysterics. It was Nellie. And I knew you had promised revenge."

She smiled, so glad that he didn't reference their kiss.

"Won't your mother be upset that you're here and not at Nellie's ball?"

"Yes, but my mother, much to her dismay, does not rule my life. I do what I want and here is where I wanted to be."

A trickle of heat spiraled through her and she smiled. She liked Levi Griffin, but she detested his mother. A more evil woman she'd never met.

The band was playing music and he took her by the hand. "Would you like to dance?"

She felt awkward. They were the only ones here, and yet, it also felt intimate. And the thought of being in his arms was exhilarating.

"Of course."

He pulled her into his arms. They had the floor to themselves and her beautiful new evening gown swished as they danced the waltz.

"You look very fetching tonight. I like the color of rose on you. It makes your dark hair look even darker."

"Thank you," she said. "And thank you for coming and telling me what had happened."

"You know, I think this is nice. It's just the two of us. We're alone dancing to a band. We can take up the entire floor if we wish. And the food you're serving looks delicious."

She smiled. "I do know how to throw a good party, when people attend."

"This is more fun, I think."

"I'm sure someone will say this is quite scandalous, just the two of us," she said. "But what else can they do to me?"

He grinned. "I see at least six other people in the room. Enough to keep me from having my way with you."

A blush spread across her cheeks and she dipped her head. No man had ever mentioned having his way with her and she kind of liked the idea. There was something about Levi Griffin that drew her to him.

She loved the way his emerald eyes sparkled with mischief, the strong angle of his jaw, and the way he smelled of something delicious. Whatever men's cologne he wore, it left her breathless.

And dancing in his arms, she felt affection she'd never experienced. Emotions she wasn't ready to explore.

"Before I leave tonight, I'm going to initiate a kiss. When you least expect it, I'm going to explore your mouth. The kiss you gave me the other night was enticing, but I want more."

A smile crept across her face that she couldn't contain. "Are you saying that my kiss wasn't good?"

The man tilted his head and gave a chuckle.

"No, I did not say that. It lacked experience and you need some practice. And I'm the man to show you how a man kisses a woman."

"Well, since you're the first man I've ever kissed, I'm sure it was more innocent than seductive," she said. "But that may change soon, if I'm to be a scandalous woman."

He laughed. "You couldn't be scandalous if you wanted to be."

"I beg your pardon?" she said, feigning shock. "I've driven through Fort Worth wearing only your shirt. I'm quite disreputable."

The music ended and he dipped her to the floor and then slowly brought her up. "Miss King, if you had not been tricked, would you have done such a thing?"

"Of course not," she said. "But maybe living like a proper woman is not in my future. Maybe I need to take on my new role more seriously. Maybe I should become the town hussy everyone thinks I am."

While she sounded like she could do this, she had no idea how a harlot acted. All her life, her father and even her servants had protected her. Until Nellie ruined her reputation, she had never even considered how a woman became an outcast.

Taking her arm, he walked her to the food table. There he gave her a plate and utensils. "And just how would you do that?"

She frowned. "I don't know. What do women who are hussies do?"

He roared with laughter. "And you think I'm going to tell you? Me, a single man?"

"Well, who else would I learn from?"

As they walked the buffet line, he filled her plate with food. It was just the two of them and his gesture was kind. Gentlemanly. Chivalrous, and she liked that about him.

"I don't know, but if I were to tell you, then I would not be considered a gentleman."

"Who's going to know? It's not like the room is crowded with people to overhear."

They came to a table and he pulled out a chair for her to sit. Why was he so easy to talk to? To ask questions, to confide in?

"All right, I'll tell you one thing hussies do," he said. "They wear indecent clothes."

She rolled her eyes at him. "Really, that's something I didn't know. My nanny preached every day of my girlhood: 'Do not attract undo attention to your feminine shape. You do not want men to think you are willing to give in to their wanton desires.'"

He laughed and she liked the deep throated sound.

"You didn't hear that kind of rhetoric growing up? You weren't warned about losing your virtue or your reputation?" She stopped and dropped her head for a moment, but she looked back up at him. "And then due to no fault of my own, except for the feeling of wanting to belong, I lost my good reputation."

His hand reached across the table for hers. "I'm sorry."

She sighed. "Oh, well, I will just find someone to give me lessons on becoming a minx. A bad girl."

"Don't try too hard," he said. "I enjoy this naïveté about you. It's delightful."

The band and the servants had retreated, giving them alone time and she was glad. It was an intimate setting, just the two of them, and she really didn't want the time to end. She liked his company. He always made her laugh.

"You should be a woman then," she replied, "and see how easy it is to be labeled. Did you grow up being told a proper young woman doesn't kiss a boy? Doesn't make eye contact with him. Doesn't laugh too loudly. Or wear seductive clothes."

"No, I was told a man takes responsibility. He gets a job that will take care of his family. He marries a fine, outstanding, upper-class woman who will bear him children," he said. "So, see, we both had to learn our proper place in society."

"No, I didn't find my place. And now, I never will."

"Don't give up just yet," he said as he squeezed her hand. "Besides, you were right."

"About what?"

"My mother tried to get me to take Nellie Robinson flowers to cheer her up the day after the ball. I refused. Nellie is the woman pursuing me, isn't she?"

"You are a quick learner," Sadie said with a laugh. "Nellie has you in her sights and she'll take out any woman who gets in her way. Even those she considers prettier than her."

"And my mother is encouraging her. Mother thinks she would make me the perfect wife," he said and shook his head.

"And what did you say?"

"When hell freezes over."

Sadie almost spewed her food. "Really?"

"Yes, I'm not marrying that shrew. I know what she did to you and I know how she reacted to your little prank. That's not what I want in a wife."

They sat across from one another, silent for a moment. Sadie so wanted to ask him what he wanted in a wife, but she knew he said he wasn't ready to marry. She didn't want to be like all the other debutantes and push him.

It just felt nice having someone here. He came out of his way to her supposed ball where no one showed up, but him. It felt nice to think he was her friend, a protector and confidant, and someone she could depend on.

"Let's dance again," he said, after they finished eating. "I'm really enjoying having the floor all to ourselves."

"All right," she said as he stood and took her hand, leading her onto the floor. The band begin to play again and they waltzed around the ballroom floor.

It felt too good to be true. To be dancing in this man's arms and yet she knew that he wasn't ready for marriage and neither was she. All she'd wanted was to have friends, and instead, she now was ostracized.

When the music ended, he led her off the floor. "It has been a lovely evening. I've never enjoyed a ball more."

She laughed. "Has anyone ever told you that you're sometimes a smart ass?"

"My dear, Miss King, did you insult me?"

"It's my new floozy personality. It's coming out," she said.

As he walked with her toward the door, she suddenly remembered his promise to kiss her.

When they reached the entrance, he pulled her outside. He cupped her chin with his hands and pulled her mouth to his. The kiss wasn't rushed or hurried. It was a slow, all-consuming movement of his lips moving over hers in a way that had her knees growing weak. And when his tongue pushed between her lips, her arms moved around his neck, pulling him in closer.

Hanging onto him to keep from falling. Wanting to be closer. Wanting more that she didn't understand.

As their tongues intertwined, her body sagged, and for a moment, she felt lost as though he was going to eat her alive, the kiss becoming more intense, creating a heat inside her that made her moan.

When he released her mouth, it took her a moment to realize it was over.

"That, Miss King, is how a man kisses a woman," he said with a smile.

Stunned, she stared at him, not knowing what to say. Only that he had ignited a fire inside her that traveled down to her center.

"Good night, Sadie," Levi whispered against her ear. "Pleasant dreams."

"Good night," she said, wondering how she could sleep after that experience.

Turning, she walked back into the house, closed the door, and stared at the musicians, the servants and the leftover food.

Now how did she top that kiss from Levi? What would a hussy do?

CHAPTER 7

*E*arly the next morning, while Sadie was drinking her coffee on the patio, her housekeeper came outside. "Miss King, there's a Mrs. Eugenia Burnett-Jones here to see you."

"What?" Sadie said, rising from the chair. The famous matchmaker had matched several ladies in town before she was caught in a matchmaking trap of her own.

The woman was legendary. Rose, Tessa, and she had spoken at length about her. But why was she here?

"Did you seat her in the parlor?"

"Yes, ma'am," Julie, her favorite of the servants, told her. "She's waiting on you."

Sadie smoothed her dress and hurried inside. Anxious to hear why the woman had chosen to visit her.

She walked into the parlor, the sun shining through the windows making the room bright. It was one of the few rooms left in the house that her mother hadn't redecorated. The woman stood. She reached out and took both of her hands in hers. "Mrs. Burnett-Jones, I'm honored you came to visit. I've heard so much about you."

The woman smiled, her hair was completely gray and she had to be approaching eighty years old. "Thank you, dear. Please call me Eugenia. After reading that detestable woman's article in the paper, I thought I must come see you. Over the years, I've checked on you and that article made me sick."

Her scandal had reached the ears of Mrs. Burnett-Jones. Was she here to help or scold her?

"Thank you, please have a seat," Sadie told the woman as she sank down onto her sofa.

"Tell me exactly what happened," Eugenia said, leaning in toward Sadie.

For the next five minutes, she told her how Nellie Robinson had tricked her. Then she told her how she had gotten her retaliation.

"I'm ashamed to say, I cut her dress, but so many bad things could have happened to me if not for Levi Griffin coming to my rescue," she told Eugenia.

The woman nodded. "You were very fortunate. Have you told the world what Nellie did to you?"

It would just sound like she was saying these things to make Nellie appear bad, plus, her own reasons were so lame, now that she looked back. She actually felt ashamed for being so gullible.

"No, I'm embarrassed. The only reason I went along with her that day was because I wanted to belong to her clique so badly. Why I believed her, I don't know, but I felt certain we were finally becoming friends."

And instead, they were now dire enemies, though Sadie was trying to step back and stay away from Nellie. If the girl would leave her alone, she would not bother Nellie. But she would never trust her again.

"That one is a rattlesnake in a female body. Everything she touches, she poisons."

It was true.

"The reason I came here today is because I knew your mother well. We were friends before you were born."

This was the first that Sadie had ever heard of this. "Really? Papa never told me much about mother's friends. He never talked about her and when I asked, he wouldn't say much."

"That's because her death devastated him," Eugenia said. "Your parents were very much in love. They were so excited about your arrival and then the unspeakable happened. Your father was just lucky he didn't lose both of you that terrible night."

Sadie was speechless. She only knew that her mother died in childbirth. "Tell me what happened."

The woman sighed.

"It was cattle drive time and your father was doing his best to finish up and get back to your mother. That spring we had horrible weather. A tornado ripped the roof off their house, causing a beam to fall on your mother which sent her into premature labor. The doctor thought you were not going to make it, but your mother held you in her arms, telling you, you must survive for your father. Then she kissed you before she bled out. No matter what the doctor did, he couldn't stop the bleeding."

Dazed, Sadie sat back and thought about what her mother had gone through. "Papa never told me any of this."

"I don't think he wanted you to know how she fought through her pain to make certain you were born. The reason I'm telling you all this is because your mother would fight for your reputation. And you must do the same."

Now, Sadie felt torn, sad actually. After everything her mother had done to guarantee her life, and she'd been ready to succumb and become wild. Why not, that's what society expected of her? All because of one incident.

But Eugenia was right. Her mother would have fought for her reputation.

"My cousin—Lord knows she's been through some trying times—would be an excellent older woman to help you adjust to your life. Fannie Tabor has been married several times. She's lived in Savannah, Georgia, most of her life. She'd been the top hostess until she got embroiled in scandal. Now she's looking for a new place to start over. And I couldn't help but think she might be just what you need."

For the last two years, Sadie had lived alone. Sure, she was lonely, but she always hoped that someday she would find the right man to marry her. After all, she was an heiress. A wealthy woman and yet no man seemed to find her attractive.

She often wondered if men didn't believe they were worthy of her, but that was completely untrue. At this moment, even before the incident that ruined her, she didn't have a clue why no man found her attractive enough to marry her.

"Will she help me find a man who loves me?"

Eugenia sighed. "She can help repair your reputation, and hopefully, a man will come forward and marry you. I will forewarn you, she's an unusual woman."

Unusual, Sadie could deal with.

With a sigh, Sadie shook her head, so confused as to what was best. "Eugenia, I wish you were still making matches. You were very good at what you did."

She smiled. "Thank you, but after I married my husband, Wyatt, I promised him I would no longer matchmake and I haven't. But this is different. I don't know if Fannie would be any good at matchmaking, but she certainly knows how to function around society. Much better than I ever have."

What did she have to lose and wouldn't it be nice to have another woman living here in this big ole empty house with her? Rose could no longer see her, and Tessa was determined to be the first woman to win the competition.

Sadie was tired of being alone and she needed someone to help her find her way in society.

"Send for her. I want to do this. Whether or not she helps me, we'll see, but it would be great to have another woman living here who I could consult with."

A big smile spread across Eugenia's face as she stood. "Well, then, Fannie should arrive soon and either you will rejoin society or who knows what she'll do. Whatever it is, I'm sure that very soon things will once again be in order for you."

"Thank you," Sadie said as she walked the elderly lady to the door. "I'm so glad you came by and told me about my mother. I so wish she were here to help me. Please, come see me anytime. I'd love to hear more about my mother."

"Your mother and I could get into more trouble. She was such a delight," Eugenia said. "To this day, I still miss her."

The elderly woman walked out the door.

Fannie Tabor would soon arrive to help her get back into society. Or teach her how to be a lady who ignored society rules. Either one, Sadie didn't care.

CHAPTER 8

Sadie was tired of sitting at home. Rose sent her a note apologizing for not being able to see her, and since Mrs. Jones's visit, she had only seen the servants. She wanted to go out to dinner at a nice restaurant.

She wanted to be seen in public. Quickly, she penned Rose a note and asked her to join her at the best steak house in town. A treat for her.

Not wanting to think Rose's father would stop her, she dressed in one of her finest gowns and asked her driver to take her to the Cattleman's Steak House.

When they arrived, Cletus, helped her from the carriage. "Ma'am, I don't like going off and leaving you here."

"Rose is supposed to join me," she said, knowing that nothing was certain, but she wasn't about to back out now. She could almost taste the savory steak in her mouth.

"I'll be just around the corner, if you need me," he promised.

She smiled at him. "Thank you, Cletus. What kind of steak do you like?"

He grinned. "A porterhouse."

"I will order it," she said.

She turned and walked into the restaurant. There were people standing in the entry, waiting to get a table. As she walked up to the man taking names, she smiled at him. "Table for two, please."

The look he gave her was so vindictive and mean, that she took a step back. "I'm sorry we're out of tables tonight and tomorrow night."

Always before they had treated her with such respect. After all, her father helped start this restaurant.

The man was rejecting her because she was a woman. A sullied woman. Speechless, she started to turn and walk away, when she heard a voice.

"Darling, there you are, did you get our table?"

It was Levi. How had he known she would be here? Had he seen the way the man gazed at her?

"They're full," she said, turning toward Levi as he pushed through the crowd to arrive at her side. "Tonight and even tomorrow night."

Levi glanced at the man. "George, surely you have a table where you can seat us?"

He knew the man?

"It's just we don't let women like her in here," he said.

"Women like Miss Sadie King? Edward King's daughter? Why ever not?"

"She's a—"

Levi interrupted him before he could say something vile. "A woman who has suffered a terrible misfortune. Whose reputation has been tarred by horrible lies being spread about her. Whose father, Mr. Edward King, was the man who made beef available to this restaurant to keep it in business."

The man's face softened. "Your father was a wonderful man."

"Thank you," she said. "If he were here, I'm sure my life would be very different." The man laughed. "And the woman who has wronged me, her father would be called out for the damage she's done."

How long would it take for the damage done by Mrs. Griffin and Nellie to recede in the minds of everyone in town? Fort Worth was not huge. In fact, it was just large enough that everyone knew everyone. And gossip spread quickly.

The man's brows raised. "Let me find you a table."

Levi smiled down at her and he took her elbow and they followed the man.

"Thank you, George," he said. "Next time, don't pass judgement."

"Yes, sir," he said, walking away.

"However did you know I would be here this evening?"

"I didn't," he said, looking at the menu. "I was on my way to dinner when I saw you standing inside here. And took a chance on sharing dinner with you."

Shaking her head, she gazed into his eyes and wanted to lose herself in him. "No, I'm buying your dinner. You helped me again."

"Whatever are you doing out alone?"

"It's been over a week since I've been out of the house, and today, I decided I wanted to eat steak. So, I asked Rose to join me, but I haven't seen her. I doubt her father would let her anywhere near me."

He reached across the table and took her hand. "I've thought about you a lot these last couple weeks."

A thrill shot through her and she caught her breath.

"And what were your thoughts?"

He grinned. "Some were quite indecent. Some were wondering how you were ever going to get yourself out of this mess. But most were about dancing that night in your ballroom, just the two of us. The feel of you in my arms and then that kiss."

A blush spread across her face. "What were the indecent thoughts?"

Laughter filled the air as he brought her hand up to his mouth and kissed the back. "A man never tells."

"Well, I just wanted to know how they compared to my indecent thoughts. You know women like me do have an imagination that keeps us awake at night."

And hers had been trying to imagine how it would feel if Levi made love to her. As a virgin, she had no idea, but she had continually thought about it all week.

"Oh, Sadie, please, we're supposed to be having dinner together. If we keep up this talk, I'll whisk you away to my hotel suite and do all kinds of deliciously wicked things to that very fine body of yours."

She tilted her head and gazed at him. "You won't tell me how to be a vixen, and then you tease with your words of having improper thoughts about me. I was just curious as to what they were. Do you want to hear mine?"

"Yes," he said softly, gazing at her in a way that made fire rip through her veins.

"We're in bed together. You're kissing me and just when we get to the fun part, I wake up," she said.

"I need a drink," he said as he ran his hand over his face.

"Was that bad?"

"Oh, hell no," he said. "But I've got to have a drink."

Just then, their waiter appeared.

"I'll have a glass of whiskey before dinner," he told the man. "What would you like?"

"I'll have the same," she said, knowing she'd never drunk whiskey in her life. "Along with a t-bone."

"Are you sure?" Levi asked her.

"Yes," she said, "I'm in training, remember. And how could one glass of whiskey hurt me? And I like t-bones."

"All right, but don't say I didn't warn you," Levi said and motioned for the waiter to bring their drinks along with the steaks they had ordered.

"You are testing yourself, aren't you?" he said.

"Why not? If I'm going to be labeled with a bad reputation, I might as well enjoy the spoils. Besides I'm getting a keeper next week."

"A what?"

"A keeper. A lady who will live with me and try to salvage my reputation. But until then, I'm tired of fighting off the gossips. Tonight, I'm going to give them something to talk about."

He grinned at her and leaned back in his chair. "I certainly hope your keeper doesn't do away with this Sadie. I'm enjoying her reckless, wild behavior."

The waiter set the drinks on the table. She lifted her glass. "To new beginnings."

Their glasses clinked and she watched as Levi tossed his down and then gazed at her.

"What are you waiting for?"

"Really, you drink the entire glass at once?"

"Yes," he said smiling. "One swallow."

She tossed the whiskey back and thought her body was in flames. She gasped for air as her throat burned all the way down to her chest and quickly reached for the glass of water.

Levi sat across from her and she could see he was trying not to laugh. "And that is why I don't drink much," he replied.

When she could finally find her voice again, she glared at him. "Why didn't you warn me harder?"

"You wanted to try a new experience. What did you think?"

The liquor had seared down to the center of her body and now she had a heat burning there.

"I don't think I tasted it at all. But it did leave my chest feeling nice and warm. In fact, it's warming me all over."

A grin spread across his handsome face and she gazed into his sparkling eyes. She loved his dark lashes, his straight nose, and full lips. The man had such nice lips. She hoped he would kiss her tonight before they parted ways. She enjoyed his kisses. They reminded her of the whiskey.

And yet, why was she so enthralled with him? Because she felt safe.

"You know," she started, "here we both are not wanting to court, but I do admit, I have fun with you. With you, I experience different things." She watched him simply nod. "The last few days, I've been thinking about that kiss you gave me. Do all kisses feel like that?"

She'd been curious if any man she kissed would make her feel like that. In a way, she hoped not, because she wanted Levi's kiss to be different.

"How did it make you feel?" he asked.

"My knees grew weak, my blood was on fire as it raced through my veins. My lungs seemed to stop working and I wanted more. I'm not certain what more I wanted, but there was something I wanted more of."

He grinned and leaned in close to her. "That's what leads to lovemaking. Kisses like that are meant to make your body long for mine. It doesn't always happen, but when it does, it means that relations between us would be magnificent."

For a moment, her heart stopped beating. The thought of the two of them coupling had been with her all week and now they were talking about it.

"Mr. Griffin," she said, leaning even closer. "I'm saving myself for marriage."

"And that's why we'll never join as one," he said.

She sat back and thought about it. "So the man who marries me will he make me feel this way?"

"Well, if he doesn't, I wouldn't marry him. That kiss we shared was about pleasure."

The way he made it sound, the joining of the two of them would be a wonderful experience, but proper women didn't do that until they were married.

"No one has ever explained this to me. Papa certainly didn't and no other woman has told me much. Just what my friends and I have concocted about our wedding nights."

Just then the waiter delivered their steaks and set them on the table.

"Oh," she said to the waiter, "would you please fix a porterhouse steak for my driver. I'll take it to him."

After the man walked away, Levi glanced at her. "You're getting your driver a porterhouse?"

"Yes, Cletus is waiting outside for me. He was worried about me coming in alone and promised he would not be far if I needed him."

Her servants were the only family she had left and she treated them with kindness. She was fortunate to have them and they took care of her.

With a sigh, she dug into her food, suddenly starving.

He held up his fingers. "How many do you see?"

"Three," she said, realizing the alcohol had affected her in a dizzying kind of way that made her tongue much looser than it should be. But she was going to eat her food and hopefully it would go away.

"Good," he said. "I was afraid I would have to carry you to your carriage and then we would have *that* scandal to deal with."

She laughed. "That certainly wouldn't make Nellie happy. After all, she plans on marrying you."

Levi finished his steak and pushed his plate away. "Now, Mother has mentioned another woman she is pushing at me. Why is it with you I feel safe? Sure, I enjoy kissing you, but you're not interested in marrying. Why not?"

For a moment, she chewed her steak in thought. "I want to marry. But I want a man who longs for me as much as I want him. And while I think you're wonderful, you have clearly said you're not interested in getting married. I'm in no hurry and when the right man comes along, then I'll marry. Until then, why can't a girl just have fun?"

"Because a woman is supposed to be actively pursuing the man she wants to marry," he told her.

"You've got it backward," said Sadie. "The man is supposed to be actively pursuing the woman he wants to marry. And, as you can see, no one is chasing after me. In fact, I've often wondered why. I'm hoping my new nanny can tell me why no man wants me."

Levi frowned as he stared at her. "Sadie. You're wrong. You're beautiful. You're so dratted stunning and you make me smile and laugh. You're exactly what I would be looking for in a wife, *if* I were ready to get married."

She leaned her head to the side and gazed at him. "And you, Levi...your kiss makes me have hot dreams of the two of us entwined in bed together. Dreams where I wake up gasping for air and glancing around the room to see if you're there. But you're not ready, and I would never push myself on a man who doesn't want me. I'm not one of those silly little gits who go to balls looking for a husband. I'm looking for a man who can't live without me."

CHAPTER 9

*L*evi had to walk her to her carriage. There was something so damned attractive about Sadie, and yet, she was right, he wasn't ready for marriage.

But if she wanted to spend some time in his bed or entwined in the sheets together, he wouldn't hesitate to snatch her up and take her to his suite of rooms at the top of his hotel.

Tonight, when she told him her dreams, he'd almost grabbed her and taken her then. The woman had him hard as rock and he knew it would take a while before he could get up and leave.

As they walked out of the steakhouse, she carried a cloth bag that held a steak for her driver. It was a small thing, but it was meaningful. She thought of her employees and tried to take care of them. He'd seen her do the same the night of the ball, telling them to take the food home to their families.

He took her hand and placed it in the crook of his arm as they strolled down Main Street in downtown Fort Worth. The late night drinking and cavorting had not yet gotten started. It was still early, but before long, the streets would be crowded with drunken cowboys.

She needed to get home.

"Thank you for sharing your evening with me tonight," she told him. "I enjoyed my time with you. I even enjoyed the whiskey. With you, I can share anything."

He laughed, remembering her gasping for air, her sapphire eyes wide with distress as she tried to recover. "Will you be drinking whiskey again with me?"

"Maybe," she said, "but it will be a sip, not a gulp."

"Good idea," he told her. "So what are your plans now? How do you intend to stay here and get along with people?"

"I don't know. I'm hoping my new lady will have some ideas. I'm also thinking of trying to do some charity work," she said. "Maybe that will make people look at me in a different light."

Somehow he didn't think so, but he didn't want to discourage her. "What would you think of us going to a ball together?"

He could see her considering the possibilities, but she wasn't certain. "If my reputation was intact, I would go with you without question. But your mother is not going to like that I'm with you and she would make my life a living hell. And what would that do to your reputation? After all, you are the man of the season. The bachelor everyone is pursuing."

The idea was inappropriate, but there was an attraction between them. Unfortunately, they wanted different things in life. And she was right; his mother would create quite the uproar. Rip what was left of her reputation to shreds in the newspaper and make his life miserable.

Not that he cared. He'd ignored his mother's tantrums before and felt certain he would do so again. But what would that do to Sadie?

They stopped in front of her carriage. "And yet, here I am with you."

"Yes," she said breathless.

The urge to kiss her was almost too much to bear. He wanted to layer his mouth over hers and show her that the other night was not just a fluke, that there was something between them.

Yet, they both recognized that neither was what the other wanted.

And her dreams of the two of them entwined in bed were almost his undoing.

She wanted a man to pursue her and show her how much he wanted her. She wanted a proposal, a ring, and forever.

And Levi was not ready for that kind of commitment. But was he ready to let another man have this woman?

That was a question he wasn't prepared to answer.

Plus, they were standing in the middle of downtown Fort Worth and probably someone nearby knew them and a kiss would create all kinds of speculation about the two of them.

But he had to touch her. He took her hands in his and leaned her against the carriage door.

"Right now, I want to kiss you with a fierceness you've never experienced. I want to make your knees give out and for you to moan and call my name. But I can't. People are watching and we both know we're not right for each other."

"True," she said in a whisper. Her hand reached up and trailed a finger down his cheek. That simple touch sent shivers through him. "We probably shouldn't see each other again."

"Yes," he said, knowing that was not what he wanted. But that it was right.

"Levi, you've taught me so much. I'll think about you often with pleasure."

Crimany, did she not realize what she did to a man? A groan escaped from his throat and his resistance melted. His mouth covered hers. He couldn't stop himself as he kissed her with all the pent-up passion that had built over dinner.

Suddenly, he broke the kiss, his breathing heavy. Unless he put her in the carriage now, they were going to find themselves using the back of her carriage. And that was not how he wanted her to experience their first time together.

Only there would not be a first time. She was saving herself for marriage and he was not.

"Good-bye, Sadie," he said as he opened the door to the carriage and all but pushed her inside. Anything to get her as far from him as possible. The woman was a danger to his bachelorhood.

She was a temptation. And he needed her gone. Even though his dick was screaming no.

"Good-bye, Levi," she said as she leaned out the window. "Take care of yourself."

"I will," he said and nodded to her driver.

If she stayed any longer, he would have carried her down the street to his hotel and enjoyed removing her clothes, one piece at a time.

But she wanted marriage and he was never marrying.

CHAPTER 10

*N*ellie Robinson sat inside the steakhouse in front of the windows where she could watch the activity on the street. For years, she enjoyed watching the cowboys, prostitutes, and fights, as the evening wore with her family.

But tonight, her mouth opened with displeasure as she watched Levi Griffin kiss Sadie. It was not a quick kiss, but a passionate one that even Nellie had never experienced and when he shoved her in the carriage, she thought for a moment he was going to crawl in after her.

"Look, Mother, look," she said. "That's Levi and Sadie."

Her mother twirled around to gaze out the window at her nemesis and the man Nellie wanted to marry. The man she had not given up on, even though he shunned her at every opportunity.

"What do you think they were doing?"

"Kissing," Nellie said. "He kissed her."

"Before that, dear," her mother said.

She wanted to scream in frustration but knew the patrons in the restaurant would not appreciate her hysterics. "What has that harlot told him? He will hardly even look at me."

"Dear, you're beautiful. Of course, he looks at you."

"No, Mother. It's like his mind is not even there whenever I speak to him. That witch has cast a spell on him and he's not even interested in me. Even after I ruined her."

The waiter tried to fill her glass with water. "Stop. I did not ask for water, and I do not want anymore."

"Yes, ma'am," the man said as he walked away.

She sat there chewing on her bottom lip, trying to think of some way she could get back at Sadie. Already, she'd done her worst, but the stupid woman hadn't learned from it, and she'd cut Nellie's ball gown. That stupid wench would pay for that.

Leaning back from the table, she glared at her family. Her father had not even noticed what they were talking about. Her mother seemed to act like it was nothing, but Nellie knew for Levi to kiss Sadie, there was something going on there.

Until she left Sadie at the springs, they hadn't even known each other. It was all her fault they even met. And yet, she wanted to make Sadie pay for that as well.

But how could she get even? What could she do?

"Who is holding the next ball?" she asked her mother.

"The Millers," her mother said, not really paying attention to her as she sat there stiff, angry and ready to fight. Levi Griffin would be her husband no matter what Sadie thought. Nellie was prettier, she had more money, and why would anyone take Sadie when they could have Nellie.

Carrie Miller was her best friend, not that she really had a good friend, but she could use her. She would send Sadie an invitation and then Nellie would be ready to embarrass her in front of everyone, including Levi.

Then he would have no interest in her. Then he would forget about Sadie and look at her once again. She would speak to his mother and get her involved.

Sadie King would soon regret the day she messed with Nellie.

"What are you thinking, dear? Please promise me you won't

have anything to do with that girl Sadie or think of harming her in anyway."

Sometimes her mother refused to consider what Nellie did to other people. She would rather pretend that nothing bad had happened and that her daughter was not involved. And so be it, if it made her feel better.

But Nellie was going to make certain Sadie never interfered with Levi again.

"Of course not, Mother. But if she's going to win Levi's heart, I think we should invite her to the Miller ball."

A frown appeared on her mother's face. "Nellie, whatever you're planning, stop it now before you embarrass this family and hurt your father's career."

Suddenly her mother was getting a conscious? What she didn't know wouldn't hurt her. And Nellie already had a plan in mind that would completely ruin Sadie. The Millers had a lovely garden that would be a perfect place for a rendezvous.

Now she just had to arrange the meeting and she knew just the man who would enjoy taking advantage of a woman.

"No need to worry, Mother. Soon, she'll no longer be in Levi's life and he'll be focused on me. Soon I'll be his wife."

CHAPTER 11

A couple days later, Sadie went to the station to meet Fannie Tabor's train. Yesterday, she received a telegram that Fannie would be arriving at four o'clock. Standing on the platform, she held an umbrella over her head to keep the sun from discoloring her pale skin.

The bustling station was filled with people meeting the arriving train. Fort Worth had only recently acquired passenger trains and sometimes Sadie had the urge to get on and never come back.

The people around her made a wide berth to avoid speaking to her. Several she recognized, but they ducked their heads to avoid her. Shaking her head, she sighed.

If only her father were still alive, this would not be a problem. Most likely, he'd be in the mayor's office telling the man he would pull his business from the city of Fort Worth if he didn't gain control of his daughter.

Nellie Robinson was meaner than a box of rattlesnakes.

Just then a tall woman wearing a beautiful hat emerged from the train. Slender, she wore the latest fashion that emphasized her figure. Her auburn hair was piled on top of her head, loosely, and she wore gloves.

She walked toward Sadie in a way that let the world know she was beautiful and in control. She appeared more to glide than hurry and she smiled at people in an unusual way. The men were given coquettish glances while she grinned at the women as if to say *watch out or I'll take your man.*

"Sadie King?" she asked as she walked up and took her hands in hers.

"Yes, ma'am," Sadie said, knowing her life was about to change. Mrs. Burnett-Jones didn't tell her how gorgeous her cousin was. The woman couldn't be more than fifty.

"Fannie Tabor." The woman leaned back and grinned. "And you're having trouble with society? Really? You're beautiful. They must be blind. All the way here, I feared I was going to be asked to restore someone I could never help. But you, my darling, will be making men drool in no time."

The woman's words made her blush and she enjoyed the feeling. Not much made her smile these days.

"Thank you, but look around at how the people avoid me," she said softly. "My father was very influential in the cattle business here in Fort Worth, and since his death, I've almost become a leper."

Fannie took her by the arm and they promenaded, not walked, across the platform of the train depot. "A young man is delivering my trunks to your home. I gave him your address."

"Good," Sadie said.

People stopped and stared at the two of them. Never before had Sadie garnered so much attention and a smile spread across her face. Fannie nodded to the people who turned to gaze at them.

"Now see, dear, just by walking across the platform how much attention we've attracted. In no time at all, we'll either resolve your problem or we'll make you the most beautiful, *baddest*, woman in the west. What are the men like here? How would you describe them?"

Levi was rugged in way that let her know he liked control, but also sensuous. "Rugged and sensuous."

"Oh, my, I like that. That makes me sweat thinking about them."

A smile crossed Sadie's face. Why did she get the feeling that Fannie was going to turn her situation on its head? And she couldn't wait to see how she did it. For the first time in weeks, she felt happiness. There was hope.

The woman stopped and turned her nose up in the air. "Whatever is that smell? It's horrendous."

"Cattle," Sadie said with a smile. "We're near the stockyards."

"Disgusting," Fannie said, pulling a handkerchief out of her reticule and holding it to her nose. She quickly changed the subject. "What is our plan for tonight?"

"Dinner should be ready when we get home. I thought you might be tired. Then tomorrow your cousin Eugenia is going to drop by."

The woman shook her head. "Oh, dear, I hope you don't think the two of us are the best of friends or something dreadful like that. Eugenia married and moved to Texas before I was out of diapers. All I know about her is that she married that dreadful Burnett man. I've yet to meet her latest husband."

Families were separated and often they never heard from one another again. But Sadie had met Wyatt years ago and he was a handsome rancher.

"Wyatt is really nice. He actually has calmed Eugenia quite a bit."

"Really?" she said, turning to her. "Well, good. She had gone a little foolish with the matchmaking."

That was the part of the story that Sadie enjoyed most. How Eugenia not only found wives for her sons, but for widowed women in Fort Worth.

"Yes, but right now, I could use her matchmaking help."

Fannie took her by the arm and then patted her hand.

"No, dear, you want the men clamoring for you. You want them vying for your attention," she said with a smile. "Now, before we go home, I want us to drive by the section of town that is where most of the society people live. Does your carriage have a top on it?"

"Yes, ma'am," Sadie told her. "The Texas sun gets blistering hot in the summer, so I've always tried to stay out of it."

"Not anymore, darling," she said with a smile. "It will have to do for now, but I'm going to shove you down society's throat. We're going to make an entrance at every party. If you're going to be a corrupted lady, then we're going to stun them. If you're going back to being a good girl, we're going to show them your innocence. Either way, we're going to make every single man in town want you, desire you, and crave you."

Sadie felt a little uneasy. "But how?"

"Leave it to me, darling. I've been thrown out of more society parties and attached to more scandal. This is going to be fun," she said with a deep throated laugh that instantly drew men's attention.

Fannie tilted her head and gave one man a wink and he tipped his hat to her. "Men are so weak. Soon, we'll have them begging for your attention."

"Oh, Nellie won't like that," Sadie said.

The woman turned and frowned at her.

"Who is Nellie?"

"The girl who ruined my reputation. I admit, I should never have trusted her. I should never have let her convince me that taking off our clothes and going bathing would be fun, but I did. But I never dreamed she would leave me naked and stranded."

The woman shook her head. "Sounds like this one is a real bitch. Don't worry, we'll fix it. Now, let's find your carriage and have your driver take us through the neighborhoods before we reach your home and I collapse."

Sadie frowned, knowing she shouldn't, but unable to stop herself. "Can we drive by the Griffin Hotel? There's a man there I would love to see me pass by."

It was wrong and she knew it, but Sadie missed seeing Levi. Missed his kisses and creating mischief with him.

The woman's face brightened. "Really? Someone you're interested in?"

"Yes," Sadie admitted. "But he's not interested in marriage."

She waved her hand and gave a small laugh. "That's what all men say until you withhold the putain and then they will do whatever you want."

"Putain?"

"Pussy, darling, pussy. You'll soon learn how to use your womanly gifts to your advantage."

Doubts filled Sadie, but she was willing to give Fannie a try to see if her methods worked. After all, what did she have to lose? Her reputation?

CHAPTER 12

*L*evi saw his mother hurrying toward him. Oh no, what now?

"Levi," she called, "a word please."

"As you can see, I'm about to go out," he said.

She frowned, her eyes started at his head and went all the way to his feet. "Who are you meeting? Nellie Robinson? Helen Davis, Carrie Miller, or any of the other fine young ladies I've tried to get you to court?"

He was not associating with any of those divas. All they were interested in finding was a rich husband who would take care of them. That wasn't what he wanted in life.

"None of them," he said. "I'm meeting Hayden Lee."

"Oh, the railroad tycoon's son," she said with a purr in her voice.

"What's bothering you, Mother?" Why he was asking this question, he didn't know.

"Did you kiss Sadie King on the street the other night in front of the Cattleman's restaurant?"

Bloody hell. Someone had seen them and reported back to his mother. Did she have someone following him? Why could he never seem to get away with anything without his mother finding out.

And no, he refused to deny what he did. That kiss had been earth moving.

"Yes," he said, remembering that night and how Sadie felt in his arms. How tempting she'd been that he wanted to jump into the carriage and do things to her that a proper young woman would blush at.

"Do you want to ruin your chances with any decent woman? That girl has been ruined. Why are you kissing or even pursuing her?"

He had asked his mother to stay out of his personal life nicely. Perhaps it was time to be more direct like a cowboy and not considerate as a gentleman.

"Because she has a body crafted by Satan that draws me like none of the other women. She's beautiful with full lips that are so ripe for kissing, full breasts that need a man's touch and hips that are meant to wrap around a man." He realized his mother was blushing and yet the words were true. They were exactly how he thought of Sadie.

"And, Mother, she wore my shirt over her naked body all the way home," he said, his voice low.

Shaking her head, she stared at him, her mouth firmed in a shocking *oh* before she took a deep breath and recovered.

"Son, I know you're trying to sow your wild oats or whatever it is young men do at your age, but you're going to ruin your chances with Nellie if she sees you kissing her again."

"Can you make that a promise?"

"What? No, but women will only accept so much from a man before they move on."

"I can only pray that will be the case," he mumbled under his breath. She refused to hear him, and once again, he would remind her of his feelings for Nellie. "Good, she can move on now. I've never wanted Nellie and I never will."

His mother's eyes widened. "You don't mean that. She's a great hostess and a beautiful young woman with all the right connections. She's perfect for you."

"I've told you multiple times. I'm not interested. Now if you'll excuse me, I've got plans with my friend Hayden. We're going to a raunchy saloon to hear a young woman sing songs about love and *amorous congress* and maybe we'll even find us a saloon girl to have for the night."

A gasp came from his mother.

Oh, how he enjoyed shocking his mother. It was wrong, but as much as she hindered or tried to, he liked giving her a real zinger that made her blush.

She shook her head. "That woman has tarnished you with her sinful nature."

"How? We've kissed and nothing else. We did share a little spit. Do you think that's what has contaminated me? I bet her saliva is so strong, it has made me crave women that are not good for me."

His mother shook her head gave him an exasperated look. "Levi, you are pushing me."

And he was enjoying every minute. "And what are you going to do about it? I'm a grown man and I have asked you several times to stay out of my love life, but you do not seem to understand those words. If you must know, it was a mutual ending between us the other night. I don't want to marry and she is looking for a husband. So we parted ways with a kiss. Does that make you feel any better?"

For some reason, Levi had become moody, his mind filled with images of Sadie since that night. As much as he agreed with their decision, it felt incomplete, like they had ended the relationship before it had a chance to begin. Like they had unfinished business.

So he'd contacted Hayden and told the man he needed a night

out on the town. Tonight, they were going to seek out women who were not uptight virginal ladies of society.

"I'm pleased to hear that, but I still think you should consider Nellie," his mother said.

Shaking his head, he walked over to the hat stand and grabbed his favorite cowboy hat. In the saloons tonight, it never hurt to look the part. Especially if they went down to the Acre where the rowdiest saloons resided.

Before he lost his composure, he needed to leave. How his mother saw anything good in Nellie, he didn't know.

"Good night, Mother. Let yourself out the door, when you're ready. And stay out of my alcohol. Drink your own bourbon," he told her with a grin.

His mother thought he didn't know about her taste for the alcoholic beverage, but she was wrong. He'd smelled it on her breath and knew that she liked to sip a good, strong drink sometimes at night.

"Good night, son. Please be careful and don't pick up any whores. They are diseased. Not someone a man of your caliber needs."

What he needed was for his mother to stop with her suggestions and leave him alone. He was a grown man who didn't need help in finding a wife. When he was ready, he would do the choosing, not her. And never Nellie Robinson. Gah!

Shaking his head, he walked out. Time to relax with Hayden and toss back a few beers before he came home alone.

There would be no saloon girls for him tonight unless he saw one he thought could cleanse his mind of Sadie.

Describing her to his mother had only reminded him of how she ignited a fire in his blood.

As he stepped out onto the sidewalk, a carriage went by the hotel of which inside he caught a glimpse of the woman in his forethoughts with another lady. What was she doing driving by his hotel?

CHAPTER 13

The carriage drove past the Griffin Hotel just as Levi stepped out onto the walk.

"Did you see him?" Sadie asked.

She wasn't certain he recognized her carriage, but he stopped and stared for a moment. It was all she could do not to tell the driver to turn around and let her say hello. She had missed him these last few days. There was a heaviness in her chest when she thought about him.

"He's a handsome one," Fannie said. "And he doesn't want to marry?"

"No," Sadie said. "We agreed that we were not right for each other. But I can't help but remember his kisses. The way he held me, comforted me."

Fannie smiled at her in the carriage. "Sometimes men don't realize what they want. They need to learn that the woman they're attracted to is not going to wait on them to make up their minds."

No, she would never push him. If Levi wanted her, he needed to court her. And then there was the problem with his mother.

That woman would drive a stake through her heart if she wasn't careful.

"No, I don't want to force Levi into marriage with me. Is it wrong to want someone who loves you? Unfortunately, Levi is not ready for that kind of commitment."

Fannie took her hand as the carriage wound its way into the upper-class neighborhood. "We'll test the waters to see. If you agree to live by my rules, we'll have you a man by the end of the ball season."

That seemed so soon. There were only a few balls left with the biggest one, the Cattleman's Ball, coming up in August.

"Even with my reputation in tatters?"

"Oh, honey, we're going to use that to our advantage. No man likes a woman who is a prude. They may say they want a pure, innocent virgin, but a woman who oozes sensuality and is confident about her appeal will get them every time."

As the carriage passed the Robinson home, Nellie was walking down the street with her friends Helen Davis and Carrie Miller, the other "mean" young ladies.

"There is my enemy," Sadie said, not really feeling proud of the fact that someone hated her so much, they would destroy her reputation.

"Smile and wave to them as we go by," Fannie said. "We want them to wonder what we're up to."

Sadie really would rather have slunk down into the seat, but she leaned out the window and waved. It was hard, but she even smiled at the trio, thinking they were probably plotting their next attack.

The look on Nellie's face was startled as they drove by. Sadie could see the confusion, the hate and the disgust as if she wanted to race after the carriage and tear the wheels off. If she had a pitchfork, she would have thrown it at them.

"Now, wasn't that satisfying?"

In a way it was, but Sadie hated to admit that she enjoyed

making the woman uncomfortable, even though she did. It would just be easier if they all got along. But that strategy had gotten her left naked at the springs.

"When we get home, I want you to make me a list of all the eligible young men who attend the balls. Then we're going to set about finding you a date for the next ball."

As much as she hated to say the words out loud, she knew they were true. "But I won't be invited."

"Yes, you will. Now, we have our work cut out for us. You're a beautiful young woman and who wouldn't want to marry a rich heiress. You see the problem is that Nellie is afraid of you. Whereas, if she had just embraced you, you both could have dominated the social scene."

What she said made perfect sense. In fact, even Nellie had suggested the reason they could not be friends was because of her beauty and wealth. Seemed perfectly silly to Sadie, but who knew what Nellie thought.

"Am I wrong to wish that none of this had happened and that we both were just two ladies vying for a suitor at the ball?"

It was true. She would have even let Nellie have Levi if they were friends before she met him. But now, they weren't friends, and unless Levi wanted Nellie, Sadie would do everything she could to stop her.

Being a *nice girl* was off the table where Nellie was concerned. She was no longer going to attempt to be friends.

Her new tutor made a grimace. "What has happened cannot be undone, so it's best if we move forward. If you let me help you, everything will soon be fine. In fact, before long, the younger ladies are all going to be very envious of you."

"What about Levi?"

"He's going to have to prove to us that he's the man for you. Time will tell as to whether or not he's willing to fight for you."

"Fight for me?"

She laughed. "Oh, honey, we're going to have men clamoring for you."

That would be unusual. Different. And as much as it sounded wonderful, an uneasiness gathered like a knot in Sadie's stomach.

"When is the next ball?" Fannie asked.

"The Millers are hosting a party next week."

The woman gave her a smile. "You may not have a date, but we'll have several men on the hook. But first, we're going through your gowns to find the most revealing one, or better yet, have a new one created."

"Revealing?" Fear traveled up Sadie's spine. What had she gotten herself into? She was one of the more modest dressers when it came to ballgowns.

"Honey, it's time to show off your assets. Make them work for you. Catch you the man of your dreams."

As the carriage pulled up in front of the home, Fannie gazed at the house and then turned to look at her, shaking her head.

"You're going to have no problems finding a man. I'm shocked they're not beating down your door. Tomorrow, that changes."

CHAPTER 14

*S*adie's carriage had driven by the hotel. Where was she going? With whom? With a sigh, he tried to push the thought from his mind. Tonight was his night with Hayden. A time for the two men to catch up.

Levi had never been one who enjoyed drinking in a saloon. They were noisy, too many not-so-clean bodies, and rambunctious cowboys looking for a fight. Sure, he'd been raised in a wild city, but that didn't mean he liked to partake of the festivities often associated with saloons.

And he was certain before the night was over there would be a fight, someone shooting off his mouth and pistol. Drunken cowboys whose egos were larger than their fists. Levi hoped he was long gone before the late night fights began.

But Hayden was enamored with a singer in the bar and Levi needed to be with his friend to keep his longing for Sadie from consuming him. Damnation, since they ended it at her carriage the other night, it was like she had invaded his mind. He couldn't stop thinking about her.

Every waking moment, she was there at the edge of his mind, tempting him, kissing him, and telling him about her dreams.

"What is this woman's name?" he asked Hayden as they sat at table near the stage. The woman was due to start performing any moment.

"Mystery Flower," he said. "And she doesn't want people to know her identity, so she wears a disguise. It's all I can do not to jump on stage and rip that mask off and see her beautiful face."

That seemed odd, because any woman singing in a saloon would be considered a disgrace. And Hayden's family who owned the largest railroad in Texas would never accept that he had fallen for a saloon woman.

"Maybe she's hiding a scar," Levi said, thinking there was another reason for hiding her face.

"No. I can't believe that. She has the voice of an angel."

Now, that was carrying it a little far in Levi's opinion, but obviously, the man was infatuated. Just like he was with Sadie. Levi pushed her image from his mind. The little moan she made when he kissed her. The way she wrapped her hands around his neck, the soft feel of her skin.

There, he was, letting her in again. Somehow he had to get her out of his mind.

They sat, sipping their beers. "Sometimes she's late. I think she likes to make us all wait on her."

Levi laughed. Now that sounded like a typical woman, especially an artist.

"Have you seen Sadie, anymore?"

Levi took a deep breath. Only in his dreams and thoughts of every waking moment. And in a carriage hurrying down the street. Where was she going this evening?

"No, we mutually agreed not to see each other anymore. She wants to find a man who will marry her and you know my feelings regarding *that*."

Hayden shook his head at him. "Why don't you want to get married?"

His biggest fear was finding out that the woman he married

was just like his mother. And yet, he loved the woman, but she drove him absolutely mad with her silly ideas.

"Have you met my mother?" he asked with sarcasm. Hayden had done his best to stay away from high-society females like his mother. Smart man.

His friend laughed. "Your mother is a lovely woman. And you know you love her."

And he did. "Yes, but do your parents tell you who is the most eligible woman at the ball and you should dance with her? Do they scold you when you dance with the woman you really admire? If I married, she would drive me and my wife to seek a separation."

Hayden grinned at him. "Do you realize what you just said? The woman you really admire? It's Sadie King, isn't it."

Of course, it was, but that didn't mean he and Sadie were going to marry. They had agreed to stop seeing each other. And right now, he wanted to ride to her house and tell her he'd changed his mind. But he wouldn't.

Just then, the crowd of men in the saloon begin to cheer and a woman dressed in a modest gown, her face covered with a black veil except for a place she had cut out for her voice to be heard appeared on stage.

"Good evening, gentleman. Sorry, I'm late, but sometimes, it's hard to get away."

Get away from what? Levi wanted to ask but knew better. She appeared gentle, calm, and even subdued. Not like the rowdy women normally encountered in saloons. This woman didn't fit in with the ladies who danced in bars.

"Tonight, I'm opening with Ava Maria."

"What the hell," Levi said out loud. That was one of the hardest songs he'd ever heard sung before. A saloon singer was going to sing that?

Hayden grinned at him.

The piano player smiled at her as he begin to play the music and then the woman opened her mouth and out came the most gorgeous sound. Hayden was right. She did have the voice of an angel. And when it came to the high notes, she hit every one.

The cowboys were either standing near the stage or sitting at tables close by and they were enthralled as they listened to her sing.

When she finished, there was a thunderous round of applause and Levi turned and shook his head.

"Exceptional talent," he said.

"I told you. She always does one song either an opera version or a hymn to open the show and now she'll sing some fun songs that the men in the audience enjoy. Then she will end the program with a hymn. Amazing Grace is my favorite."

"Now, let's have some fun," she said, smiling as she walked across the stage. "How about Yankee Doodle Dandy?"

The music belted from her mouth and Levi leaned back and let the music flow over him. For the next hour, she kept the audience enthralled. They sang, they laughed, and she even did a little dance while Hayden stared at her.

Levi would admit that she could sing, but why was she wearing the disguise? Who was she?

"Gentlemen, it's way past my curfew and I must get home. Tonight, I'm going to end the show with a request that we all be kind to one another. Help your fellow man."

She bowed her head and began to sing Amazing Grace and Hayden grinned at Levi.

"Told you," he said.

Something about that voice got to him. He'd heard it before but could not place exactly where. But this wasn't the ordinary saloon girl. This woman was special.

As she finished singing, the men jumped and hooted and hollered as she walked from the stage, blowing them kisses.

After she left, Levi shook his head. "That was not what I was expecting. When you think of a saloon singer, I think of a seductress in a skin tight, low-cut dress. She was covered more than my mother."

It was true. She didn't dress like a songstress, but rather a woman who knew how to sing, but wasn't allowed to.

"Man, it's all I can do not to run up on stage and yank that disguise off and find out who she is. I'd like to lock my mouth over hers and show her how she affects me."

Levi laughed. "I thought I was hopeless. But you're worse."

"I know. And can you see me bringing a saloon girl home to meet Mother?"

A chuckle came from deep inside Levi. "Yes, I certainly can. Of all the women, it's only Sadie I'm interested in."

"And for me, it's the mystery flower. And don't even think about approaching the stage. You see those two big burly men. They will haul your backside out the door. I know because I tried."

CHAPTER 15

A week later, Sadie sat in the parlor with a young man named Anthony James. She had met him once or twice at the previous balls, but never really showed any interest in the man.

Now she realized he was interested in her. Shame, she didn't feel the same. The man was handsome, nice, and so boring, she was having a hard time staying awake.

Fannie had been giving her lessons in flirting and even modified some of her clothes to be more fitting for a tantalizing young woman. Mainly, the tops of her breasts were more exposed.

"Anthony," she said with a little laugh, "you know a woman never reveals who she's kissed. Why do you ask for such scandalous information?"

"You've not seen the paper, have you?"

A trickle of alarm went down her spine. "What are you talking about?"

"Mrs. Griffin's column. She wasn't happy about you kissing her son," he said. "I know he's the man of the summer, that all the women are chasing. Are you after him, as well?"

Blazes, could that woman not find anyone else she wanted to abuse?

Leaning over, she picked up his hand. "Anthony, Levi helped me in a very delicate situation. We're friends."

"Then why did you kiss him?"

Dash it all, someone must have seen the two of them on the street that night when Levi walked her to her carriage from the restaurant. He'd warned her that someone would see them kissing. But his mother? Did she watch his every move?

"It was actually more of a good-bye kiss. Of us parting ways as friends."

The man considered her words. "Why in damnation would he let you go?"

Oh, how, she wondered the same, but he wasn't ready for marriage. Instead, here she sat with a very nice man who bored her senseless. The fourth one this week. And all of them she compared to Levi, though she was doing her best to break that habit.

She smiled at him and removed her hand from his. "That you will have to ask him. He's not looking to ever marry and I'm not in a rush, but I am searching for a man whose company I enjoy, we have fun together, and wants to pursue me."

Anthony's face brightened and he smiled.

"Are you that man, Anthony?"

No, he wasn't, and she knew it, but she was being nice. Though she was quickly getting a headache from playing the coquet. It was tiring.

"Believe me, I'm not one who attends teas, but for you, I'm here to find out if there's an attraction. I'm in no hurry to marry, but like you, I'm looking for someone to spend my life with."

At least, they seemed to both be looking for the same thing. But it didn't feel right. There was nothing here that excited her, made her knees go weak, or even her heart beat a little faster.

She gave him a timid smile, and per Fannie's instructions,

turned so he could see the swells of her breasts. When she moved back, the poor man's eyes were glazed. It just seemed so unfair and she was tired of the game.

With a quick glance at her watch pen, she smiled. The poor soul looked like he was ready to pass out. "I'm sorry to cut our time together short, but I must get to the dressmaker. I'm having a new gown made for the Miller ball."

"That's day after tomorrow. Do you have an escort?"

A smile crossed her face. He was the third man to ask her. The other two had been told no and she intended to tell Anthony no as well. For this ball, she was going alone to let the other men see that others pursued her.

"I'll see you there," she said. "Be sure to save at least one dance for me."

"Bloody hell, I'll make certain you have my entire dance card," the man said, his eyes glazed with lust from which she had to hide her shudder.

She grinned at him and rose from the settee, indicating the tea was over. These meetings were tiring, and frankly, she was bored with them. The four men who had attended were rather boring compared to Levi.

But she refused to compare the men to a man who would never marry.

"Thank you for coming, Anthony," she said softly as she walked him to the door.

The man grabbed her hand and raised it to his mouth. "The pleasure was mine. I can't wait to see you at the ball."

"Thank you, good-bye," she said as he walked down the steps to the street. A bounce in his step.

Fannie came rushing in. "How did it go?"

With a sigh, she shook her head. "Why do I compare them all to Levi? Anthony was a perfectly nice man, but he didn't make my knees weaken or even bend, for that matter. In fact, he was rather boring."

A smile crossed her tutor's face. "Come, we need to get to the dressmaker. I can't wait to see you in that gown."

"He asked me to the ball," she said. "But I did like you said, I told him I would see him there."

"Great," Fannie said. "Oh, and I'm going to accompany you. Everyone needs to see that you have a chaperone. Someone to watch over you."

Not that the woman could keep her safe. She wasn't big enough to manhandle a cowboy. But Sadie wasn't worried. Her servants kept an eye out.

As they walked to the waiting carriage, Eugenia was coming up the sidewalk.

"Fannie, I thought you would come see me?"

"Eugenia, I'm busy," Fannie said. "Ride along in the carriage with us. We're on our way to the dressmaker."

Eugenia climbed into the coach with them. "Ladies, I came by to talk to you about some of my tricks I used when I was a matchmaker. Don't know if you can use my help, but many a man has been caught by cooking a casserole for him."

It was all Sadie could do to keep from laughing. The thought of her cooking would be enough to scare most men off. She didn't know how to cook. No one had ever taught her.

"That's not a bad idea, Eugenia," Fannie said, gazing at Sadie.

"Oh no, I don't have a clue how to boil water. I've lived with servants all my life."

The carriage hurried down the street and the women swayed side to side. Outside, a late afternoon thunderstorm poured rain from the heavens.

"True, but if we had a delicious spread and a ball, I'm sure we would get lots of partakers."

The memory of her last attempt at a ball overtook her. And she felt Levi's arms around her as they danced the waltz on her ballroom floor, just the two of them. That night had been magical as he kissed her goodnight.

"No, I had one right after the event and the only person who came was Levi," Sadie said softly. "I was so embarrassed."

"Oh, don't worry about that, dear. You and I both know I would be able to get lots of people there. Including some interesting characters," Fannie said, laughing as she patted her cousin Eugenia on the hand. "Did you get me that list of people who have been excluded from society."

Oh, dear, people who were in the same situation she was in. People who for some reason were now excluded.

"Yes, I did. There are about twenty names on there and I'm sure they would love a second chance."

"Great. We'll announce our ball at the Millers' on Saturday night. And don't worry, Sadie, we'll have a great group of people attend."

But Sadie couldn't help but worry. Not only were they inviting people with tarnished pasts, but would anyone else show up? This time, she didn't even think Levi would attend.

"What about Mrs. Griffin?"

"Oh, yes, she'll be invited as well. Now, let's try on that new gown."

CHAPTER 16

"Now, Levi, you know who I have recommended you dance with tonight," his mother said, sitting beside him in the carriage. For a semblance of harmony, he felt the urge to try to mend their relationship. But that didn't mean he was going to abide by what she wanted.

"Mother, have you ever considered that by pushing me toward these women, you do them no service. I'm going to dance with whom I please. If they strike me as interesting, I shall ask them for a twirl on the floor. If I don't, I will not waste our time."

This was why he normally took his own carriage, plus, it meant he could leave when he was ready. She liked to socialize and gossip to the very end and he liked to leave when he was bored.

In the carriage, he could feel her tense. "Well, at least you're not seeing that Sadie King any longer."

There it was. The way his mother buzzed like a gnat on a hog. Constantly pestering. And why had he thought that tonight would be any different from the countless nights he'd been with his mother?

The carriage pulled up in front of the Miller house. A glorious new mansion set on the bluffs looking out to the west. Not far from Sadie's home. He wondered if she would be here tonight. He hoped she would be.

Just the thought of seeing her again made him happy and drained the tension from him.

"I am going to dance with Sadie tonight," he said as he stepped out of the carriage.

His mother placed her hand in his, her mouth pursed tightly. "You wouldn't dare."

"Oh, yes, I would dare. In fact, I'm very much looking forward to it."

Why did she care who he danced with? It was none of her business.

"You said you went your separate ways," his mother said, wrapping her grip around his arm as they walked to the house.

"We did, but that doesn't mean we aren't still friends."

With a sigh, she shook her head. "She's going to trap you."

Good grief. Sadie was not the one he worried about deceiving him. Nellie was the one he had to be aware of.

"No, you are the one to trap me, Mother," he said.

She turned and stared at him. "Whatever do you mean?"

"You are going to do something that will force me into marriage, and when you do, you will not be happy with the consequences."

"I would never do such a thing," she said.

"Perhaps, but your little list of available women would."

He felt her stiffen and knew he had made her angry.

"They're acceptable, high-society young women," she said. "You'd be lucky to marry any of them."

When they walked into the ballroom, his eyes immediately went to Sadie standing with a woman he didn't know and Eugenia Burnett-Jones and her husband Wyatt.

"Excuse me, dear, I have people to see," his mother said coldly. "And, no, I'm not talking to someone to trap you."

"Wonderful," he said. It had been a mistake to come with his mother. But he had been trying to be a good son. Sometimes that embroiled him into even more trouble.

Trying not to let Sadie know how much he wanted her, he danced first with one girl and then another while she laughed and flirted and danced with several men. Rumor was that her new chaperone was lining up men to court her.

And as much as he hated to admit, he didn't like that idea. All-fired, how he had missed her.

From the corner of the room, Nellie watched, and every time he passed her, she would smile and bat her eyelashes at him. The woman was dangerous.

Finally, unable to resist any longer, he walked over to Sadie. The woman's dress was beautiful, stylish, and incredibly seductive. Her breasts were pushed up and over, lowing the top almost to the point of being indecent. And a long slit ran up the dress to expose her leg.

It almost looked she had intentionally dressed to be seductive.

"Good evening, Sadie," he said as he stared at her. "Would you like to dance?"

"Yes, thank you," she said with a demure smile.

If he had his way, he would take her home right now and lock her up so no other man could see the way her body was revealed. He'd seen more and knew how those gorgeous white legs looked even higher.

"New dressmaker?"

"Yes," she said. "I'm making changes in my life. If I'm going to be accused of being a loose woman, then...you know the rest."

That was not what he wanted to hear. "Who gave you that advice?"

"My new tutor, Eugenia's cousin, Fannie Tabor."

What could he say? He had no right to admonish her or tell her that she was courting trouble.

"I'm sure your mother will put me in her column tomorrow. You saw the one about our kiss?"

"Yes," he said, enjoying too much the feel of her body in his arms, but wanting to take off his shirt and cover her once again.

"I hope you know what you're doing," he said. "Be careful. A dress like that draws the attention of men who are ruthless."

They whirled to the sound of the music and he knew the song would be ending soon causing a sadness in his heart.

"Levi, I've thought about you all week."

"As I have you," he said, wondering if she felt the same emotions he did. What were they doing? If they both were thinking about each other, that meant they were not finished. Not yet anyway.

"But we both know you are not ready for marriage. And I'm tired of being alone," she said. "We've been over this. We should never have danced, because it's just torture for the both of us. And I need to focus on other men. Men who want me."

She was right. But, dash it all, he couldn't seem to resist her. The music came to a halt and he walked her back to her side of the room. His heart shattered. This was not how he wanted their dance to end.

"Good evening, Miss King." He kissed the back of her hand with a bow.

"Good evening, Mr. Griffin," she responded with a short curtsy.

They were so formal. Almost to the point of appearing cold to one another. While inside his chest, his emotions were mush from the pain of trying not to think about her.

He glanced across the room and Nellie gave him a saucy look. Why the hell not? He knew she was a woman he would never marry. In her arms, he was perfectly safe.

Walking across the ball room, he smiled at her. "May I have this dance?"

"Of course," she said with a giggle.

Why did she seem so immature? They walked onto the dance floor and she took his hand. "Thank you for the dance," she said.

"You're welcome."

"All night long, I've been waiting and watching for you."

Well, perhaps this wasn't a good idea after all. "And?"

"Now you've finally gotten around to dancing with me. Your mother invited me for tea tomorrow. Will you be there?"

Oh, damnation no, he wouldn't be there. What was his mother doing?

"I'm sorry. I had heard nothing. She didn't mention it to me and I am meeting with the hired staff of the hotel."

It was a lie, but he wasn't having tea with her and his mother. He would create a meeting if he needed to. Or even better, he would ride out of town to clear his head for a while.

Women made him want to escape from the drama.

Out of the corner of his eye, he saw Sadie go into the garden with A.J. Williams. The man was a bootlicker of the vilest type. Aggressive and uncouth. Just the sort of man to do his best to take advantage of her.

Nellie gave a little giggle as he glanced toward the door. She'd seen Sadie and A.J. go outside.

He stopped dancing and frowned at her. "What's funny?"

"Nothing," she replied as she tried to pull him back into her arms and begin to dance again.

His feet refused to move and he gazed at her. "Excuse me, but I think I should check on them."

Her face turned white. "No, don't go out there. Let's continue dancing."

"Why? What have you done, Nellie?"

Her brows raised. "Me? I don't know anything."

"You're lying," he said, leaning into her face, with a scowl.

Something was about to happen and he felt certain it wouldn't be good for Sadie. He dropped her arms and hurried off the dance floor, all but running to the door.

When he pulled it open, Sadie was fighting. She drew back her fist and hit the man in the nose, but he was determined to finish ruining her.

"You know you want it, you little bitch," he said, pulling at the front of her dress.

Anger gutted Levi as he took two steps and grabbed A.J.'s suit. "No, she doesn't want anything from you."

He doubled his fist and hit the man knocking him out cold.

"Are you all right?"

She fell into his arms. "No. This is not what I want."

Wrapping his arms around her, he pulled her in tight to him. Holding her, his heart pounded in his chest. This felt like where she belonged. In his arms, no one else's.

"Sadie, what am I going to do with you?"

She leaned back and gazed at him, tears streaming down her face. "Take me home. Now."

"Absolutely," he said. "Let's walk around the outside of the house and we'll take my carriage."

As soon as he had her in the transport, he told a servant to tell his mother he would return for her. And he would, but first he needed to see about Sadie. Make certain she was all right.

CHAPTER 17

*S*adie felt like the biggest fool. Once again, she'd been betrayed, and this time by a man. The ugly words he'd said to her made her heart ache.

Now, as she rode in Levi's carriage, she wondered if she were to blame for what happened tonight.

"He didn't hurt you, did he," Levi asked, sitting beside her, patting her hand, his arm wrapped around her, holding her. She felt so safe in his arms.

Just the smell of him made her heart swoon and her knees buckle. And the way he had gone after A.J. left her warm. No matter the situation, Levi seemed to always protect her.

But he wouldn't always be by her side. He didn't want to be.

"No, he said some horrible things to me. Told me he was going to show me how a slut deserved to be treated. Told me I was a cunt and he would enjoy making me his whore."

She felt Levi tense, but he didn't condemn her.

"I think Nellie was behind it," he said. "We were dancing and she was almost giddy. I have no proof, but she did try to stop me from going after you."

That would be about right. The woman was obsessed with her. She wanted to ruin her for good, so that no man wanted her.

The carriage hit a pothole. The streets of Fort Worth, Texas, were dirt and after a big rain they often had craters in them.

"I don't know why she's after me. I've done nothing to her."

"Except cut her skirt," he said with a laugh.

"That was only after she left me at the springs, naked. Seemed fitting, at the time. Now I feel like I'm in a war that will never end."

"She'll soon get bored," he said.

She leaned her head against his shoulder. "Fannie said I will either be accepted or we will ramp up my unacceptable status. I'm not much of a suggestive female." He chuckled. "I'm doing my best, but Fannie has strange ideas."

They pulled up in front of her home and a shiver went through her. She didn't want him to leave her. She liked the feel of him holding her in the carriage, his arms protecting her. And yet they were home.

"Would you walk me to the door?"

This was the end. She knew he would no longer be her rescuer. He would no longer be the one she could turn to for help. She needed to become strong and cease depending on him.

"Of course," he said. "I shall come in and make certain everything is fine."

He stepped out of the carriage and turned to help her alight. "You know, I really do like this dress."

"Thank you, but the cut skirt revealing my leg was a little much. I don't mind showing off an ankle, but a knee is more than I'm accustomed to."

A grin spread across his face. "Well, I've enjoyed gazing at your knee all night, but then I've seen it before."

A blush crossed her face sending warmth through her. Once again, he'd rescued her and she didn't want tonight to end. With a sigh, she started toward the house.

"Yes, you have."

She took his arm as they walked. "Sometimes I think I'm not going to attend anymore balls. Just have my friends over and forget about finding a man to marry."

It was true, she was so discouraged by being in society, she just wanted to stay home. "That way no more revengeful acts will befall me."

"Why are you so keen on getting married?"

"I'm alone. This big old house all to myself. And I want children. A family of my own with more than just one child. You're an only child, didn't you get tired of all the focus being on you?"

And she'd missed out on having a mother. Someone to guide her through her girlhood years.

"Yes, and I regret it to this day that I don't have a brother or a sister. Someone to focus Mother's attention on rather than just me. So much is expected of me and sometimes it becomes too much."

His mother...would she put tonight's episode in her column? Once again, showing how Sadie had created scandal? Right now, she didn't care. At the moment, she felt so discouraged that she just had to get through the good-bye with Levi.

"Yes, I understand completely. Before Papa died, he was telling me what was expected of me. But now that he's gone, I miss him. If he were here, I don't think I'd be having the problems I am with Nellie. Or maybe I would."

They came to the door and she pulled out her key. The servants would be in bed or in their quarters by now. She opened the door and turned to him. "Thank you for once again rescuing me. A.J. was a brute and if you hadn't come out when you did, he would have…"

He put his finger to her lips. "It's over. And I promise you, he will never bother you again. I'm just glad I arrived when I did."

She gazed up at him and so wanted to kiss him but knew they shouldn't. Yet, she was drawn to him. Something about the way he smelled so clean and masculine. His strong muscles, his twinkling bright green eyes and firm jaw. The strength of his embrace. The feel of his arms.

Unable to resist, she stepped forward and he met her halfway. Their lips collided and he wrapped her in his arms, his mouth consuming hers. With a whimper, she leaned into him, feeling his strong body molded against hers.

This was who she wanted. Levi.

His arms felt like heaven and she wrapped her arms around his neck, squeezing even more into the kiss.

Suddenly, he pulled back, gasping for breath. "I can't get you out of my mind and this doesn't help."

"Agreed, but your kisses take me to another place. One where I see us together."

"And therein lies the problem, my dear."

With a sigh, she knew he was right. She stepped out of his arms. They wanted different things, no matter what their bodies were telling them.

"I'm giving up on being with you. Tonight, we both know it will never happen," she said. "So I'm walking away from you, Levi Griffin."

He grabbed her hand and brought it to his mouth. "If you ever need me, you know where to find me."

She nodded. Fighting to keep the tears at bay, knowing if they started, she feared they would never stop. Her heart was crying out for this man and she suddenly realized the reason she was having such a hard time letting him go was because she loved him.

"It's time I found another knight in shining armor."

A grin spread across his face and he stepped back off the porch. "Take care, Sadie."

"You too, Levi," she said as she watched him hurry to his carriage, taking a piece of her heart with him.

When had she fallen in love with him?

She watched as he crawled in the carriage and the driver spurred the horses as it pulled away from her house.

"Sakes alive, Levi! I wish you felt what I do."

With that she turned and walked into the house. Alone again.

CHAPTER 18

"You disappeared last night," Fannie said.

Sadie sat with her new housemate in the garden having breakfast and drinking coffee. Sadie had slept very little last night and this morning she wanted to go back to bed and nurse her broken heart.

"That's because A.J. all but tried to ruin me in the garden. Levi came to my rescue and then took me home."

A smile crossed Fannie's face. "Excellent. I remember seeing A.J. coming in with blood pouring from his nose, but I didn't know what happened."

Why did she seem so pleased? Was the drama that happened in the garden a good thing? Had the woman never been attacked before? The man had inserted his hand in the front of her dress and tried his best to rip the bodice, but she had kicked and clawed her way until Levi arrived.

"He's not welcome here any longer," Sadie said. This morning she had awakened thinking of Levi and wondered how she could consider any other man. Even though she knew their relationship would never work with him not wanting a wife.

But she was also no longer willing to accept fools. And A.J. was a fool she never wanted to see again.

"So let's plan our ball," Fannie said, her face perking up with excitement.

"I'm not certain I want to hold a ball," Sadie said. "Who would come?"

Fannie laughed. "I'll send out the invitations. Believe me, it's going to be interesting. Not a boring event like last night."

Was she mad to be listening to this woman's advice? Last night's ball had ended in a disaster after she wore a dress that had the room abuzz with gossip. Though Sadie had felt uncomfortable in the scandalous dress, her tutor thought it wonderful.

And it had attracted attention, just the wrong kind.

"Your dress was a hit last night. It had the old maids' mouth dropping and the young girls envious of you."

"And it almost had me ruined," Sadie said, again thinking of the terms A.J. called her. She gave a shudder thinking again, what if Levi had not arrived in time to help her.

"But who saved you? The man I know you want," Fannie said with a smile. "Sooner or later, he's going to come around."

No, he wouldn't. After last night, she felt certain she would never see him again. They were too much of a temptation to each other. They needed to keep apart or find themselves in trouble.

"I don't want to force him. If Levi decides he wants me, then that will be wonderful."

"And you shall have your wish," Fannie said with a smile. "There is more than one way to bring a man around."

Just then the maid appeared, a crushed look on her face. "Miss Sadie, someone dropped this off on our doorstep this morning."

A frown crossed Sadie's face as she took the envelope from her servant. "Thank you, Janie."

Tearing into the missive, a newspaper article fell out. Mrs. Griffin's article. Just what she didn't need this beautiful morning.

At the Miller ball last night, Sadie King appeared in a dress that only a trollop would wear. The low-cut bodice showed off the swell of her breasts and then the silk fell to the floor with a ruffled slit all the way to her thigh. When she danced, you could catch glimpses of her legs all the way to her knees.

And the men were enamored of her. Until she went out in the garden with one particular man and never returned. What happened to the fair Miss King? Did she escape the ball with her lover?

Will there be a wedding announcement soon?

Hopefully, that will be the last we see of this young woman who has fallen so far since her father's death.

Meanwhile, the ever popular Nellie Robinson and Miss Carrie Miller danced until the wee hours of the morning, chaperoned properly.

"Strumpet," Sadie said out loud.

Fannie gasped. "Let me read it."

She started to laugh as she read the column. "I wonder if Mrs. Griffin has any skeletons in her closet. I may just have to make some inquiries."

"No, her son is Levi," Sadie said. "I know they have a difficult relationship and I don't want to cause any trouble between mother and son."

Though she hated Mrs. Griffin, she loved her son, and the thought of them arguing or fighting because of her was more than she could handle. She knew he loved his mother, though he often grew frustrated with her.

"All right, but I don't think it would hurt to see if we can learn anything on her. Also, Nellie...surely. Has the evil child done something in her past that would cause her trouble?"

A bee flew to the hyacinths, pollenating the flowers. "Now that woman, you can dig up all the dirt in Texas and I would gladly help you spread it across town."

The two women laughed.

Then Fannie leaned forward in her chair. "Now tell me, did Levi kiss you goodnight?"

The memory of them coming together, the heat, the passion

the feeling of want was like a pain in her chest. Last night, she realized she loved him and would do whatever she had to, to protect him.

"More like kiss me good-bye. We again agreed that we were not right for each other." Seemed like she'd said those words once before.

Fannie smiled. "We'll see about that.

"If we're going to find you a husband, we need to get to work," Fannie said.

The image of Levi came to mind and she pushed him out. They were not meant for one another. Though her heart told her something else.

CHAPTER 19

*L*evi spent most of the day thinking about Sadie, trying to push the thoughts of her from his mind, but she refused to leave. The kiss on the porch she initiated all but consumed him. He could not forget the feel of her lips, full and tempting being pressed against his.

For just a moment, he wondered about how she would be in bed. Would she reveal to him she really was a bad girl? Or would she be a virgin, innocent of what happened between a man and a woman?

The thought left him eager to find out. And he had to press down the urge to pursue her regardless of his fears.

"Levi," his mother called as she entered his suite, "are you here?"

"Yes, Mother," he said. "Give me a moment."

They were going to have dinner in the hotel. And tonight, he was going to remind her of how much he disliked her interference in his life.

Pulling on his western suit coat and hat, he walked out of the bedroom, just in time to see her toss something into the fireplace.

"What are you doing?"

The woman startled. "Oh, I didn't need that card any longer, so I decided to just burn it."

She was lying.

He walked over to the fire and retrieved the envelope addressed to him. Opening it, out came a smoldering invitation to a ball at Sadie's home.

Glancing up at his mother, he shook his head. "This is not your mail or your invitation. You have no right to destroy it."

She sighed. "You're right, but I received one today as well. You need to stay away from that hussy."

"Don't call her a hussy. She's someone I care about." He was tired of her disparaging Sadie.

"Well, I'm not going," his mother said in that indignant tone of voice he detested.

"All right, then I can go and not have to worry about what you're going to write in that dreadful article you compose for the paper."

Her mouth opened and she started to speak, when he held up his hand.

"I was waiting until we were at dinner, but this discussion is better suited here. Sit down, Mother."

Her eyes widened, but she dutifully sat on a horsehair couch. Her green eyes narrowed and he could see her wall of defense rising, preparing for battle. And he hadn't even said a word yet.

"As my mother, you've always looked out for my best interest. You've protected me from the time I was a baby until my late teens," he said, watching a smile form on her face and her defenses lower.

"But I'm twenty-six. I've built a good business here in Fort Worth and I no longer need you coddling me."

A frown crossed her face, her eyes narrowing and he could see she wasn't happy with what he was saying.

"If I decide to court Sadie King, that will be of my concern.

No one else's." Where had that come from? All night long, he'd thought about Sadie.

Her mouth dropped open. "No, son, she's not good for you."

"I'll decide who and what is good for me, do you understand?"

"Just not Sadie," his mother said, shaking her head. "Nellie or Carrie would be better for you."

"Give me your reasons against Sadie." He wanted to get to the bottom of her hatred now and dispel any misbeliefs. Not that he had decided to court her, but then again, why not? They were obviously very much attracted to one another. Why not explore this growing attraction? He'd been thinking of it for days and last night just confirmed his thinking.

"Son, you rescued her when she was found skinny dipping in the springs. You saw what she did to Nellie's dress. And now that woman, Fannie, has moved into her home to help her find a husband. And last night, it's rumored that A.J. and her were fornicating in the garden. A decent woman, a proper mother of your children, does not do that."

There were so many lies, so many mistruths, and yet how did he convince her that what he knew was true? It would be his word against hers, and once again, Nellie was spreading lies.

"Mother, Nellie Robinson is a vicious woman who will do anything to make Sadie look bad. *She* left Sadie at the springs. Took off with Sadie's clothes and returned to town, leaving her naked and alone. So many horrible things could have happened to Sadie because of her."

"That's what she gets for skinny dipping," his mother said, turning her nose up at the very idea.

"What if I told you that Nellie persuaded her to remove her clothes and go swimming? That Nellie engaged her to skinny dip with her and then left her there."

"A decent young woman does not do such a thing," she said, suddenly appearing bored. "Besides, look what she did to Nellie's dress. Cut the entire back out of it. Leaving her so embarrassed at the ball."

No matter what he said, she refused to listen to reasoning. The truth was right in front of her and she still wanted to believe the lies that Nellie had spread.

Taking a deep breath, he shook his head. "But it was all right for Nellie to leave Sadie naked."

His mother was impossible to reach.

"Last night, while I was dancing with Nellie, she knew that A.J. intended to accost Sadie. No, Sadie did *not* have sex with him in the garden. When I got out there, A.J. was attempting to force her into a compromising situation."

Her eyes widened. "*You* hit him."

"You're damn right, I did. Then I took Sadie home," he said with a sigh. "Mother, surely in your life, you've experienced something where a man tried to go too far with you?"

A strange look crossed her face and then she adamantly shook her head. "No. I was always the well-behaved girl."

Something about the way she refused to look at him as she said the words made him doubt her. Could this be the reason she was so adamant about him marrying a socially-accepted girl? Had she encountered a troubling situation in her life?

Could it have something to do with his father? The father he never met. The father it sometimes felt like didn't exist?

Where was the evidence of his father? Their home never had pictures of the man or anything that showed they were married. He'd been thinking about this for months and it just seemed too convenient.

Suddenly he turned to her. "Mother, where are pictures of Papa?"

She licked her lips nervously and sighed. "They are put up in a trunk in the hotel's attic. I'd have to heavily search for them. Why are you asking?"

"I was wondering where they were. I don't remember what

my father looks like. I've never seen a wedding picture of the two of you. Nothing in your home is reminiscent of Papa. Did I have one?"

"Of course, you did," she said agitated. "It's painful to look at him and know he's been gone for so long."

Her response didn't sit right. It felt like she was just frustrated that he was asking about tomfoolery.

Finally, she threw her hands up. "I'll try to find them for you," she said. "Now, are we finished arguing and are you going to escort me to dinner?"

"That depends on you, Mother. Are you going to be acquiescent to me asking Sadie to dinner?"

There was silence for a moment. "Son, I would be satisfied if you asked anyone *but* her. For my sake, my son, ask either Nellie or Carrie to Sadie's ball, and if you do not enjoy yourself, then I'll accept your decision."

She wanted him to take a woman she approved of to Sadie's ball? The woman he intended to ask to dinner that very night? So many things were wrong with that idea, that he didn't even know where to begin criticizing. He was exhausted of her shenanigans.

"No. How could you ever think that would be acceptable to me?" The woman did not give up. "Mother, when I look at Sadie, my heart thumps louder; my hands sweat and I dream of her. Something is tugging me to her, and as much as I don't want to marry, I've decided to find out what this draw is between us before it's too late."

Her eyes widened. "Just don't marry her."

Confusion suddenly swelled within him. He didn't want to marry but *why was that?* When he thought of Sadie, this attraction, this drawing as if his soul needed her, consumed him. And that made him wonder if she *was* the one for him to marry.

Right now, he needed to make certain they were compatible elsewhere than the shared desire for each other.

"I'm not making such promises. And if I choose her for my

wife, which is completely *my* prerogative, and you refuse to accept her as your daughter, then we will wish you well in the rest of your life."

Her mouth dropped open and she stared at him. "Sometimes you remind me of your father."

"Excellent. I'd like to see a picture of him, please."

CHAPTER 20

*L*evi's friend Hayden attended Sadie's ball with him, and true to form, his mother had not shown at her ball. Maybe that would be for the best. Then she could not write a column denouncing anything that happened here tonight.

The place was filled with unfamiliar faces and Levi had to search the room a few minutes before he located Sadie, making certain the food table had plenty for everyone. She looked breathtaking tonight with her hair piled in curls on top of her head, a dress that revealed more than he approved of, and a faint smile on her face.

His body demanded he get her alone, but he knew he would have to wait. First, Rusty Smith whisked her out on the dance floor.

A band played a lively song and he smirked to himself that Rusty was not the best dancer. But Sadie followed as best as she could. Soon after that, another man asked her to dance and he noted he would have to get in line if he wanted to dance with her tonight.

"Wouldn't it be great if the Mystery Flower was here," Hayden said, glancing around the room.

"You dream of the unlikely, my friend. The crowd would notice someone wearing a mask."

"Yes, but what if she's here and she's unmasked. That's my goal tonight, to be near all the ladies, perhaps have them sing for me to see if I can locate her."

Levi started to laugh. "Your heart is so deep, you can't see your boots. How do you think your high-and-mighty family will react to learning you're yearning for a lady who makes her living singing in the saloon?"

"The same as your mother discovering you wish to be bollocks deep in Sadie," he said with a laugh.

That was no lie. During the past several days since his discussion with his mother, he had made a momentous decision. He had yet to see a tintype of his father, so today, he hired a Pinkerton agent to learn about the man who birthed him.

It occurred to him that he didn't even know the date of his father's death or what he died from. And after his mother's reaction the other night, he was beginning to have doubts that the man even existed.

What if he were illegitimate? Could that be one of the reasons his mother insisted he marry someone from society. Even though in Fort Worth, Texas, high society was merely people gathering to dance and be social without going to a saloon. Yes, there were many who were quite wealthy, but there were also those not so rich.

Standing off to the side, he watched as Sadie danced with several single men, spending no extra time with them, always making certain each man maintained a respectable distance.

Could she really be a seductress? Her kisses screamed innocence and yet there were several instances that belied her being a shy, virtuous, young lady. What if his mother was right?

Did he really care?

Her dress tonight was cut low, and once again, she had a slit up her dress that exposed her leg. A slit that showed her knees as she danced. Though the dress was beautiful, he wanted to explore exactly where that slit led too. And if they were courting, he would tell her to save those dresses for him. Only him.

But at the moment, she wasn't his.

"Stop the music. Stop the music," A.J. Williams said, standing in the middle of the ballroom.

A trickle of unease spiraled down Levi's spine. The man's eye was still bruised where Levi had punched him the other night. If he caused trouble tonight, he would give him a matching bruise on the other eye.

The band stopped playing and the crowd around him parted.

"Where is Sadie?" he called.

She walked into the center of the ballroom, her shoulders back, looking like a woman prepared for battle, and Levi had no doubt Sadie would make him pay if he spoiled her party.

He took her hand and pulled her close to him. "I'm here to apologize for the other night. Your beauty overwhelmed me, and after our kisses carried us away, I took advantage of you by lifting your skirts and touching you intimately. Today, I thought it would be best if I came and offered you my hand in marriage. I love you and just in case there are consequences, I think we should marry."

The crowd gasped and Sadie tossed her head back, laughing, a blush spreading across her face. The lickfinger was trying to make it sound like he had gotten away scot-free with what Levi had stopped him from doing.

Snickers were heard behind him and he whirled round to see Nellie and her cohorts giggling. He still believed the little witch had put A.J. up to this, and now it appeared the man was still doing her bidding.

"Consequences? Of what?" Sadie called out. "You trying to manhandle me? The only thing that happened was Levi answering my cries for help. The reason your eye is blackened is because he punched you for not stopping when I told you no."

"Will you marry me?" A.J. stuttered out, looking around as if to find assurance this was what he was supposed to be doing. This whole charade was meant to embarrass Sadie. He knew she would never agree to marry him, but this way, he had shamed her in front of everyone at her party.

"Yes, I'll marry you," she said, stepping into his face with an expression to scare away any hornswoggler.

For a moment, Levi's heart stopped, but then he realized she had accepted to put him on the spot. And it was working.

His mouth dropped open and he glanced around the room almost looking for an escape route. "But…"

"You did this to embarrass me in front of my friends. Nothing happened in the garden. And your little ploy is not going to work. Who put you up to this?"

The man licked his lips nervously. "Sadie, you know how it is between us. The earth moves when I kiss you."

"The only thing that moves when you kiss me is your lips and tongue, and it's rather disgusting. Like I told you in the garden, a man who tries to overpower a woman and force her is never anyone I would consider husband material."

His face turned red, and he became angry. "Don't worry. I would never marry a loose girl like you."

Sadie grinned. "Oh, the bloom of love has already faded. Leave before my friend Tessa puts a bullet in a specific area of your body."

The woman appeared at Sadie's side, a pistol twirling around her finger and stopping in her hand, prepared to fire.

Tessa Harris's father ran a smithery and he was an excellent gunmaker. She'd been raised around firearms and was a perfect shot. Tessa had been Sadie's friend since their school days and he knew she would defend Sadie.

A.J. turned and stomped out of the house, his face flushed, his body stiff. For a moment, Levi had thought he would have to give the man a second warning about staying away from Sadie, but she'd taken care of the matter.

Agitated whispering came from behind him. "Somehow, she always escapes. How does she keep doing that?" The growl the young woman elicited was quite unladylike.

"I apologize, folks, for that little scene. Levi can verify that nothing happened in the garden at the Millers' ball the other night. A.J. tried and he failed. Now let's get back to having fun."

Levi turned around to gaze at the group of women who were whispering. "If I speak to A.J., is he going to tell me that someone put him up to doing this tonight to embarrass Sadie? Is he going to tell me that someone convinced him to attempt what he did the other night?"

He glared at each female individually. "If I find out someone was behind this, I'll have my own column in the newspaper talking about how some women are hideous on the inside. And that type of woman would *never* be my wife."

"Levi," Nellie said, walking up to him, laying a hand on his arm, "you know Sadie is a scandalous woman. None of us have to coerce a man into trying to take advantage of her. She is quite willing."

"Nellie, you have been trying to ruin her for months. But I'm warning you. If I find out you're behind this, I will let the world know what kind of woman and wife you will be. And something tells me you three women are involved."

With that, he whirled around and went in pursuit of Sadie. After searching through the main areas of the house, he found her outside in the garden, staring up at the full moon.

"Here you are," he said. "I've been looking everywhere for you."

"Sorry, I needed a little break after that scene."

"Which you handled very well."

"Thank you, but how many people are going to believe me?

Everyone would rather think I've done something outrageously wrong. It fits my image much better than the real me."

He pulled her in his arms. "I like this Sadie. I believe I like the bad girl image even better. She's to the point and outspoken about her feelings. Tell me, when I kiss you, are my *lips and tongue the only things that move?*"

A laugh escaped from her and then she glanced up at him, her eyes darkening. "No. More. So much more."

He grinned. "Excellent. That's what I wanted to hear."

"Why do you say that? You don't want me," she said, her voice a whisper in the darkness.

"I have never said I didn't want you. But after the last couple of days, I've come to the realization that maybe instead of instantly saying no, we should explore this connection between us."

She tilted her head and frowned at him. "What made you change your mind?"

"My mother. From the moment she learned I picked you up at the spring, she has done nothing but harp at me that you are not what I need. But what if she's wrong? It's time for me to make my own decision regarding being with you. Maybe we'll soon realize this was never meant to be. Or who knows what could happen?"

Sadie shook her head. "Mr. Griffin, if you intend to court me, you have to work for the privilege. Especially, after all the drama your mother has made me go through."

"That I can do," Levi said as his mouth came crashing down on hers. It was as if she let down her resistance as she wrapped her arms around his neck, pulling him closer to her. While his mouth moved over hers, his tongue danced around her own, causing her to moan deeply in her throat.

As fire sped through him, he felt her crushed breasts against his chest and he longed to lay her on the outside table and make her truly into a bad girl. To claim her and mark her as his own. But that would have to wait.

He needed to stop before things got out of hand, but he couldn't resist kissing her, exploring her mouth, dreaming of having her.

Suddenly, a pie came flying down from the second story of the house, landing on top of them, splattering their clothes, clinging to their hair.

"What the damnation?" he said, breaking off the kiss.

"Nellie," Sadie said with a laugh. "She seems to know how to interrupt and cause havoc in the best moments."

Levi started laughing and yelled up at the window. "Nellie, thank you for the pie. Lemon, my favorite."

Carefully, he wiped the moisture from Sadie's face. "Close your eyes," he said as he scooped the pie and then moved it over her lips. She licked his fingers and he thought he was going to hell for such thoughts that invoked.

What Nellie didn't know was that she had made this moment almost magical.

"Cook made this pie," she said. "I would know her recipe anywhere."

She blinked open her eyes and then she scooped more of the pie dripping from his hair. She licked it off her fingers and smeared what was on his cheek into his mouth.

"I'm really enjoying have dessert with you," he said laughing.

"Me too," Sadie said and then she leaned forward and kissed him again. This time, she reached around and grabbed his buttocks. Pulling him in even closer. While Levi was stunned she would be so forward, he also knew that he liked how she went for what she wanted. Him.

When they broke apart, Levi felt as if he were standing in the flames of hell. It was all he could do to keep from taking her right there.

"Now that was a very sweet, sensual kiss," she said softly. "One I'll never forget. Tell your mother to write that in her column."

Laughter spiraled through Levi and he reached down and

kissed her on the nose. "Let's keep my mother out of our heated kisses."

She shrugged and smiled. "If you insist."

"Come, let me take you into the house and cleaned up."

"She's not going to ruin my party," she said. "I'm not going to let her."

But when they returned inside, most of the guests were departing.

Fannie came running up to her. "What happened?"

"Someone dropped a pie on us outside," Levi told her.

"The same someone who told everyone that the cook had died and it was time to go home?"

"She didn't," Sadie whispered.

"Oh, yes," Fannie said. "She did. And then everyone began to leave."

Levi sighed. Once again, Nellie had managed to damage a party that Sadie held. Between her and his mother, he was beginning to wonder what they would do next. Especially when they learned he was courting Sadie.

CHAPTER 21

*T*he next morning, Sadie awoke to thoughts of Levi. Their kiss in the garden had left her wanting more with this man than anything she'd ever experienced. And now he had changed his mind about courting her. But did this mean he was serious about marriage?

She wasn't certain what had happened, but for some reason, he made his intentions very clear. Now, to see how he intended to carry them out. For her, his actions would tell her if he was serious about exploring this attraction between them. Since the night he rescued her in the garden, she had been in love with him. That there was no other man she was interested in, but that didn't mean she was ready to find a preacher. For now, she just wanted to see if her feelings were true.

And when the pie fell on them, startling them, it had the opposite effect Nellie wanted to bring about. Instead of causing an angry scene, the filling of the pie ignited their hunger for each other. The pie became a sensuous aphrodisiac that inflamed their kisses and their passion even more. Certainly not the effect Nellie had intended to initiate.

Today, Sadie intended to write her a thank-you note, telling her she had made their moment together even more special. That the pie was delicious and she was so glad that she shared it with them.

That would kink her pantaloons.

Jumping up, she couldn't wait to get downstairs and talk to Fannie about the ball last night. After checking to make certain she had removed all the lemon from her hair, she twisted it up in a knot and dressed.

When Sadie entered the kitchen, Fannie sat reading the paper.

"That Mrs. Griffin is despicable. If I ever see that woman in person, I may slap her. For a woman who didn't attend, someone filled her in with juicy gossip."

Sitting at the table, Sadie watched one of the servants bring her coffee. Could Levi be telling his mother what happened? But the way the woman twisted the situations into something they weren't, Sadie could not believe that.

"What does she say?" she asked, fearful of what the woman had said to make Fannie want to slap her.

Last night, Miss Sadie King, was proposed to by A.J. Williams III after their indecent encounter in the garden. A.J., ever a gentleman, did the honorable thing of asking her to marry him, but our scandalous miss, she turned him down. And then proceeded to meet another mysterious gentleman outside, where they were spotted kissing. When will she ever learn, or will she disgrace herself until there are consequences to her actions?

"That wench," Sadie said out loud. How could she consider Levi as a husband when his mother hated her? And why? What had she done to this woman to make her hate her so much?

"She is something else," Fannie said. "I've never seen someone so vindictive. And she doesn't even know that the mystery man you went into the garden with was none other than her son."

Sadie laughed. "And if she knew what we did out there, she'd be mortified. When the pie fell on us, we incorporated the filling into our kiss. Our wonderful kisses. I even licked some of the filling off his face."

Fannie started to laugh. "Maybe you should tell her the next time you see her. *Oh, by the way, your son's kisses are lemony sweet.*"

For a moment, Sadie almost snorted her coffee. "I was thinking of sending Nellie a thank-you note. *Dear Nellie, thank you for dropping the pie on us last night. We licked the filling off each other's face.*"

Tears came to Fannie's eyes as she howled with laughter. "Do it. I think it would make the perfect ending to her trying to destroy your ball. Why does she hate you so much?"

"We've been enemies since grade school. She never liked that my father was just as rich as her father. Not that I knew what that meant. Over the years, I've tried to be friends and every time I got burned. Some people are simply not meant to be liked. Funny thing is, I feel sorry for her. She is more fixated on being mean to me than making her own life happy."

Just then, Julie, one of the maids came into the breakfast room carrying the most beautiful bouquet of flowers. "Ma'am, these just came for you."

"Oh my, they're so pretty. Set them down and let's see who they're from."

Julie placed them on the table and Sadie knew the moment her hand touched the card. "To a beautiful woman who I enjoyed sharing lemon pie with last night. Please join me for dinner tomorrow night at the hotel."

A smile crossed her face and she read the card to Fannie and Julie.

They both smiled.

"And how are you to reply?"

A frown crossed her face. "I want to have dinner with him, but his mother hates me."

Julie slipped from the room and left the two women pondering what to do. How could she and Levi have a life together with his mother interfering? And did she know that her son planned to court her?

"What if he's the man for you? What if the two of you are perfect for one another? Why would you let this crabby old woman come between you?" Fannie asked.

A bluebird flew outside the window dive bombing the other birds who tried to come into the garden.

"Just like that bird out there," Fannie continued, "this woman is overprotective of her son. Why are you going to let her win, especially if you care for Levi? Last night, the other gentlemen didn't have a chance. You danced with them, but once you saw Levi was here, you became different."

"How?" Sadie asked, wondering if it showed that she loved Levi, that she knew he was the only one she wanted.

"No longer were you available. Yes, you danced with the other men, but you were waiting for him until A.J. made a scene."

Sadie realized what Fannie said was true. She'd been waiting for Levi to approach her and he did after A.J.'s proposal.

Betty Griffin was overbearing and could be the reason that Sadie could never be with Levi. But what if Mrs. Griffin came to accept her? Perhaps she was the kind of mother who couldn't accept *any* woman being in her son's life. But for the moment, Sadie had to try.

"Right now, I'm going to take things as they come. I want to court Levi, to know him better to see if he is the man for me. Then, together, we'll deal with his mother."

"The way the two of you look at each other, oh yes, he's the man for you. I thought the room was going to catch fire last night. Especially while he watched A.J. His fists were clenched and he was ready to defend your honor."

Sadie laughed as she glanced at the flowers. They were

wonderful. What a thoughtful way to send her an invitation. What a grand way to remember last night.

"Excuse me while I write out my thank-you note to Nellie and also a quick note to Levi. Now what dress shall I wear to dinner with him?"

CHAPTER 22

*L*ater that day, Nellie opened the front door and accepted a card from the delivery man. Usually this meant she was receiving an invitation to a ball or something exciting. But when she opened the card, she gasped. It smelled of lemons.

Dear Nellie,

I am sending a note to thank you for dropping the lemon pie on me and Levi last night while we were kissing. Once again, your actions brought us closer. We met because of you leaving me at the springs. But last night, our attraction grew even stronger as we shared dessert in the moonlight, kissing the juicy pie off each other's lips. Thank you for making our relationship grow.

Sadly, when we returned to the ballroom, most of our guests were leaving after being told the cook had died of some kind of poison. And, of course, I do believe you were the instigator of A.J.'s attack on me in the garden and then asking for my hand in marriage last night.

And who is telling Mrs. Griffin what to write in her column in the newspaper? I'm thinking it must be you. It is quite a shame you are unable to accurately retell events. Perhaps you could practice memory games to enhance your appeal to suitors.

Every day, I think you'll come to your senses and stop this nonsense, but not yet. When is this going to end?

Sadie

Rage filled Nellie as she screamed and tore the note into pieces. "You harlot. You're not going to keep him."

CHAPTER 23

 evi had thought about dinner with Sadie all day long. He had reserved a private dining room and he looked forward to spending time with her alone. That evening as he dressed, he heard the door to his suite open.

"Levi, are you home?"

If he ever were to marry, he would need to either find a home or make certain his mother did not just drop in. What was he thinking? He didn't want to marry. Why would he?

"I'm in the bedroom," he said. She walked in. "Well, thank the Lord, I am dressed, Mom."

"I birthed you. I've seen you naked."

"Things have changed."

"Where are you going?" she asked, staring at him.

"I'm having dinner with someone," he said, not wanting to let her know with whom.

Her eyes narrowed in that all knowing way mothers have. "Did you read my article in the paper today?"

He turned to face her. She seemed almost gleeful and happy. What had she done now?

"No, should I have?"

She grinned. "You didn't go to Miss King's ball, did you?"

"Hayden and I both attended," he said.

A frown furrowed her brow. "So you saw the proposal."

Staring at her, he gave a snicker. "Worst proposal ever."

"What? That's not what my resource said."

Somehow he needed to find out who this *resource* was that kept giving her fallacious information and put a stop to it. He'd even considered contacting the paper and telling them they were promoting false information.

"Well, they lied. A.J. almost received his second black eye from me. And when Sadie accepted his proposal, he about wet in his pants. Not that she meant it. But she knew it would scare him, and it did."

A stunned look appeared on his mother's face as she shook her head. "No, no, that's not what I was told."

Something about the way her expression alerted him that she'd written some very salacious things about Sadie. Maybe it was time for her to face the truth. Bollocks, he'd be the one to enlighten her.

"Two nights ago, I stood in Sadie's garden and told her I wanted to court her. I made no promises, and I'm not even certain we'll see each other after tonight, but, Mother, I'm going to to pursue this attraction between us."

Her emerald eyes grew large and her mouth dropped. Then he could see the anger gripping her as she clenched her fists, her eyes flashing. "But, son, she's a bad girl. She's loose and wild and she's not worthy of you."

"Mother, you say those words, but I see no evidence of them."

"Have you not been reading my column in the paper?"

"No, I try not to. I'm not one for gossip. I believe on facts. What I behold with my own eyes," he told her as he pulled out his stopwatch. "I've to go. My dinner date awaits."

His mother sighed. She knew she was not going to win this

argument and he'd warned her about interfering. Maybe she was accepting reality.

"She is not good enough for you."

"Maybe *I'm* not good enough for her," he said with a smile. "Good night, Mother. Please show yourself out the door."

Levi was not standing here any longer to let his mother ruin his night. He could hardly wait to see Sadie and spend time with her. They had much to talk about and learn from one another.

As he left the suite, he wondered if he should have walked his mother down the stairs, but he didn't want to risk Sadie and her seeing each other. The two women were like oil and water and never appeared to mesh. And he needed to know why.

But tonight, he wanted to focus on Sadie and hear as much about her as he could. And at the end of the night, he would take her to her home and kiss her soundly. In fact, that kiss spurred him down the stairs to his waiting dinner date.

When he reached the dining room, he saw her sitting, waiting for him. She was breathtaking. For a moment, he watched her and couldn't decide if he wanted her, or food, for supper.

The dress she wore was more subdued than a ballgown. But the bodice was tight and caused the swells of her breasts to spill over. Demurely, she sat, unaware of the attention of other men who stared at her beauty.

He stepped to her side and she gazed up at him, her sapphire eyes sending a thrill of warmth through him. All she had to do was stare at him with those large eyes and dark lashes and he was hers. And when she added that full lipped smile, he melted.

"Good evening," he said.

"There you are," she said with a smile.

"Do you think I wouldn't come tonight?"

"I feared perhaps you had been *called away.*"

"No, I'm all yours tonight," he told her, taking her hand, lifting her to her feet from the bench. Then he placed her arm on his as he led her into the room he had reserved.

She wore a light perfume that he breathed deeply of, enjoying the light freshness of her scent. Her hair was up, exposing her neck, and for just a moment, he wanted to lean down and kiss that bare spot.

He pulled the chair out for her and she sat and then he hurried to sit across from her. A bottle of champagne sat in a bucket on the table. Champagne was hard to acquire, but his hotel had a few bottles set aside for special occasions.

"Champagne?"

"Yes," he said. Why did this night feel special? Especially after his discussion with his mother.

She raised her brows. "Is there something you need to tell me?"

He laughed. "No, but this is our first official courting night, and well, I thought it was special."

A grin spread across her full, so very tempting, lips.

"You said you wanted a man to pursue you. I'm pursuing."

"I did say that," she almost whispered. "I'm glad. Tell me about yourself. All I really know is that your mother writes the most egregious column in the paper. And that you own this very fine hotel."

A waiter appeared and opened the champagne before he disappeared.

"I'm working on changing my mother from writing such horrible trash. Someone filled her head with nonsense about what happened the other night at your ball."

"This morning, I read your mother's column. It was laughable, it was so wrong."

"I haven't read it. But I don't want to talk about my mother. I'm here to learn about you."

"And me, you," she said and the most delicious whisper of desire pulsed through him. As he stared at her, his heart pounded in his chest and his dick was stone.

He held up his champagne glass. "To learning about one another tonight."

"Yes," she said. "To learning what kind of man you truly are."

He grinned at the thought of her wanting to find out about him. No other woman had really been interested in *him*. They wanted his money but were never intrigued in him as a man. Sadie had her own money.

They each sipped from their glass, her eyes staring into his.

"You were saying about yourself…" she said.

"After college learning in the east, I realized Fort Worth didn't have a luxurious hotel. So I built several smaller hotels first, to learn more about the business and to see if there was even a need for a grand hotel. When I was twenty three, I started construction on the Griffin Hotel. There is a small suite for my mother and I have a suite on the upper floor."

"It's a beautiful hotel," she said. "The most magnificent building in town. But what made you want to build hotels?"

It was a question no one had asked him before and it made him admire her even more. She truly wanted to learn about him.

"They are the fastest way to make money in our cow town. Couples and families don't want to stay in the Acre and witness the madness in that section, so I built my hotels on the west side where you can view the prairie. Except this one, which I built closer to downtown and the river."

The waiter came to their table. "Sir, are you ready to order?"

"Give us a few more minutes," he said.

They glanced at their menus and then he looked at her. "The steaks are always good, but the chef is from Italy. I snatched him up when I met him in New York. It took me a while to convince him he would love living out west."

"What do you recommend?"

"The spaghetti Alfredo. It's not your typical restaurant meal," he said. "At least not here in cow town, and it's our most popular dish."

She closed her menu. "I'm trusting your judgement."

"Good."

After the waiter had taken their order, she reached across the table and took his hand. It was a confident, sure response, and let him know this was a special night for her to be so open and free with her emotions.

It also made him realize just how strong a woman she was to not only have grabbed his buttocks and pull him in closer, but to reach across the table and hold his hand. He liked the connection.

"Do you enjoy building hotels or was this just a way to make money?"

Another great question. For a moment, he tried to remember who had asked him about his love for buildings before now and could not think of a single person.

"Oh no, I love to build things. Hotels, schools, hospitals. Anything that the community might need. It's my way of giving back. We moved here when I was five from the East Coast. My mother wanted to get away from the big cities, my father's death, and well, she wanted to start over. Her family was dead and there were only the two of us."

Strange that he remembered nothing of the journey out here. Only what his mother told him. And now he had doubts about his father. Soon, he hoped the Pinkerton man would find out something on him.

With a squeeze of his hand, she released him, but he wanted that simple touch that connected her to him and he grabbed her hand again. Holding it tightly, not letting go.

A smile spread across her lips.

"Once before, we talked about we're both only children," she said with a grin, "do you want more than one child?"

It was true. He'd never really considered it before, but they had that in common. No brothers or sisters. Not even a nearby aunt or uncle. They were both alone and it was then he realized that was not the kind of life he wanted.

All his life, he'd been envious of his friends who had lots of siblings. Even his friend Hayden had three sisters and two brothers. That's what he wanted—a big family. A house filled with laughter and happiness.

And yet, he kept telling Sadie he didn't want to marry. Was it just an excuse to keep his mother at bay? She had the worst taste in women.

"I'd like a big family. With daughters and sons and a wife I adore by my side."

"Then why did you tell me you never wanted to marry."

A laugh escaped him. "It's a cop out. A way to keep women at a distance, I guess. A way to keep the leeches my mother likes away. Only with you, I have been torn. There was something about you, and after we kissed, I wanted to know more. After I rescued you, I knew I could not put it off any longer. I had to know more about you."

The bad girl, as she was known, blushed and he knew she wasn't as scandalous as they called her.

"What about you?" he asked. "What do you want in life?"

"My mother died in childbirth and I only had my nanny and father. No aunts and uncles, no one else. So I'd like to have a big family. Lots of children. A husband who adores me. I'd like to create a home filled with love. One that when I'm old and gray, I can look back at what we created and think 'well done.'"

Why did it feel like that was exactly what he wanted? Like they both were looking for the same thing.

"Are you ready to get married?" he asked to see if anything had changed in her wants.

"If I find the right man. I'm looking for someone who will, as my daddy told me, make my knees go weak when he kisses me. Who looks at me and we understand exactly what is being said. And I'm not willing to settle for less. I can wait or do without. Regardless, I'm in no hurry, but yes, I want to get married eventually."

At least she didn't appear to be rushing them to a church. She honestly wanted to make certain they were right for each other.

The waiter entered the room, carrying their dinner, and for a moment, they were quiet as he set the plates in front of them.

After he left the room, Levi smiled at Sadie. "The chef knows I'm here tonight, so this should be delicious."

She took a bite and then moaned. There was something about a woman who moaned over her food that let a man know she would be great in bed. That she would be noisy and full of life. A woman that with each passing moment, he ached for.

"Tasty?"

"Wonderful," she said with a smile.

They ate in silence for a few minutes and then, he asked the question he'd been wanting to ask for a long time.

"So, Scandalous Sadie, tell me, are you really a bad girl?"

She started laughing so hard she had to put her napkin up to her mouth. And he knew the answer before she even answered.

Finally, she stopped giggling and smiled at him. "That, sir, is for you to discover on your own. I would think that a man in some ways would like a bad girl in secret, but he wants the world to think of her as a good girl. I'm not telling. You'll have to find out."

CHAPTER 24

*S*adie had never been on many outings with a man and
never a dinner in a private room, but tonight had been
so much fun. They had laughed and talked and told each other
private, intimate thoughts. Things she'd never shared with
anyone, but now, she really must be getting home. It was late.

"Come up and see my place before you leave," Levi said,
holding her in his arms. "The view of the city is quite romantic,
especially at night."

The dinner had been cleared away and now they were
standing in the doorway.

"It's only a few floors away."

"Your mother is not there, is she?"

"She better not be if she wants to continue living here," he
said.

A grin spread across Sadie's mouth and she wasn't ready for
the night to end. No, it would not be proper for her to go into a
single man's living quarters without a chaperone, but she was
already considered a floozy. What was one more nail in her
reputation?

"All right, but only for a moment," she said. "And then I must be getting home. I don't want to be out anywhere near the Acre this late."

"We'll be quick," he told her.

Levi grabbed her hand and they rushed through the restaurant and up the stairs. Three flights up, he took a key out of his pocket and put it in the lock.

When he pushed open the entry way, she walked inside. It was a lovely place with a living area and small kitchen. Big windows overlooked the skyline of Fort Worth. Immediately she walked to the large glass panes.

"Astounding, how did you put in these windows?"

He laughed. "It was difficult and I was scared that one of the workers would be killed, but I was right there, telling them how to install them and we accomplished the task, all fingers and toes still attached."

"Look, you can see the saloons in the Acre. The gaslights on the street and even the carriages with their lit lanterns traveling the road."

She felt his arms slide around her as he came up behind her and pulled her in close. "It's even better in the morning when you can watch the sun rise."

His lips moved along the side of her neck and down her bare shoulder sending tingles of awareness right to her middle.

"This is nice. The dinner, the view, and now standing here with your arms around me."

"I agree," he said, his lips moving along her neck as she leaned against him and let him kiss her.

"I don't want you to stop."

A chuckle came from deep in his throat. "I don't want me to stop either," he replied, holding onto her like he would never let her go.

Whirling her around in his arms, his lips moved over hers again and he kissed her like it was their last. His lips ravaged her and she met his fervor and clung to him, his body close to hers.

The man had rescued her from A.J., he'd watched her as she spurned the man's proposal, and soothed her when pie landed on them. He'd rescued her from the springs and he was the only one she thought of, dreamed of, and wanted.

Tonight, she needed him. Right this moment, she desired him like her next breath.

Whatever this was between them, she wanted to know more. To experience where this would lead them.

With her hands, she pushed open his shirt, wanting to touch his skin, feel his chest. For weeks, they had danced around one another, neither one sure of the other, but tonight had proven they wanted the same things. That they were drawn to each other with this incessant need driving them together. No more. She wanted him and she wanted him now.

If she were to be labeled, then she would let him experience her innocence. Let him teach her how an experienced woman responded to a man.

She ran her hands over the feel of his hard chest muscles, his flesh rippling beneath her touch while his lips continued their assault on her. Her breathing was labored and an ache began to build between her legs.

Their lips broke apart. "Lord, I want you so much," he said, his hands caressed her head, holding her tightly.

"And I want you," she said, her breathing harsh in the glow of the lantern.

"We can't," he said breathlessly, wrapping his arms around her. "Sadie."

"Stop talking. I'm here. I'm willing and I want you. Show this bad girl what it means to be a woman."

Pulling out of his arms, she began to unbutton her dress, pulling it over her head. Was she really doing this? With no promises of tomorrow, no wedding ring, nothing but trusting her instincts?

Her heart pounded in her chest, pumping blood through her

veins and she knew she was taking a risk, but she didn't care. She was alive, she was breathing, and tomorrow her "soiled" label would at least be true.

"It's time," she whispered.

As she stared into his emerald eyes, glassy, shining with a fire that drew her to his flame, a shudder rippled through her at the knowledge of the chances she was taking, willing to accept whatever risks their joining brought.

Frantically, before she could change her mind, she pulled his shirt out of his pants. While he undid the buttons, she pulled the garment from his body. When the shirt was removed, he reached up and grabbed her head, bringing her lips to his again. His lips conveyed a message of desire and longing, and oh, sweet Lord, want. She opened her mouth greedily, accepting his unspoken acknowledgment of passion.

Their lips broke apart and he placed his mouth on her neck as he nibbled softly to the curve of her shoulder. "Are you sure?"

"Love me now," she whispered in the glow of the lantern. She knew for certain that this moment she needed Levi. She yearned for him.

Lifting her in his arms, he carried her to his bedroom, kicking the door closed behind them. When he set her on the bed, he lifted her chemise, tugging the garment over her head, exposing her breasts.

"Perfect," he said as he lowered his mouth to her puckered nipple, tenderly sucking the tiny bud. A burst of fire flooded her and she gasped, throwing her head back, arching her chest into his mouth. The sensation flooded her with desire for this man.

His hand gripped her breast as his tongue lavished her nub, filling her with a sweet ache that seemed to radiate all the way to her toes. Gently, he pushed her onto her back before he stood and began to remove the rest of his clothes.

Rising onto her elbows, she watched while he removed his pants, his long johns, and his boots. Even in the dimness, she could see him in all his naked glory. His manhood jutted out from his body like a weapon looking for a shield.

"So that's what a naked man looks like," she said softly.

For a moment, he tilted his head and she could see she had confused him. But that wasn't the only surprise.

He reached down and slipped her shoes from her feet. They fell to the ground with a clunk as he slid her stockings down her legs. His fingers reached for her pantaloons and she lifted her hips to help him remove the garment.

Lying naked before his eyes, she began to doubt her decision. Nervous, she watched his gaze travel over her breasts, her hips, and then back.

"The glimpse of your body at the lake is nothing compared to the beauty I'm drinking in now. Tonight, I will make you mine."

A thrill traveled through her at his words. This was what she wanted, what she longed for. A joining of their bodies since he already owned her heart. And soon, she hoped he would acknowledge he felt the same way. That he loved her.

She was giving herself to a man who she wasn't certain loved her, but the passion between them needed to be explored. The fire growing inside her must be extinguished, and he was the only person who could douse the flames. She needed Levi.

He crawled up on the mattress until they lay side by side, their naked skin touching. His lips covered hers once again, and the heat that had been simmering, burst inside of her like an explosion of flames, sizzling her from head to toes.

Sadie ached to touch him, to feel his skin beneath her fingertips. She trailed her fingers down his face, to his chest, feeling the hardened muscles beneath her touch. His muscles rippled beneath her strokes and she slid her fingers down his waist to his manhood.

He wrapped her fingers around his cock and he moved her hand up and down. She gripped his erection, touching the tip, feeling the bulbous head on the end of his shaft.

She'd never seen a man's penis before, let alone touched one. For a moment, she was in awe of the power and the strength in his erection.

At the touch of his fingers between her legs, she gasped at the zing of feelings that radiated from her center. She moaned as his fingers caressed her intimately, touching her like she'd never been touched, creating a need she'd never experienced. He stroked her until she was wet with want and filled with a raging desire that had her arching against his hand.

"Levi," she gasped, not understanding what was happening to her. But unwilling to stop and ask questions.

His lips covered hers, raking the inside of her mouth with his tongue teasing and dancing, retreating and withdrawing while he shifted his body over the top of hers.

She knew what came next, had dreamed of being with the right man. Was Levi the right man for her? That remained to be determined. But he was perfect.

He guided his penis to her entrance and then surged ahead, powerful and yet tender--and met a wall of resistance.

"You're a virgin?" he said between clenched teeth. "You're not a bad girl, at all."

"Make me your angel," she demanded.

Levi pushed forward, she felt the barrier give way, and cried out as pain replaced pleasure.

He paused for a moment. "Just breathe, it'll soon pass."

In a matter of moments, the pain subsided and she felt certain she could continue. That she had to know what happened next.

She reached up needing him to continue, wanting this man to finish what he'd started. She pulled his mouth to hers and then she moved her hips.

He groaned as he moved within her. He drove himself into her body and she welcomed each thrust. Heat spiraled through her, building each time he plunged into her with an intensity she'd never known.

"Levi," she moaned, "what's happening?"

His face was tense and full of pleasure, his eyes boring into hers, lifting her and carrying her with him. "Sadie."

She met his thrusts with equal force, each stroke spiraling desire higher and higher in her, pushing her toward some unknown peak. Then the wave crested and she could feel herself falling, tumbling, and plummeting. Falling as her body stiffened and shudders shook her deep to her core. Levi's mouth locked onto hers as he held her, thrusting into her one more time as his body tensed around her.

He released her mouth and slumped down over her. "Oh, Sadie."

She lay there panting, her body slowly recovering, as she was amazed at what had just happened. He rolled off her body, still holding her close. His breathing slowed and he held her, his eyes closed, his chest rising and falling.

"Why didn't you tell me you were a virgin?"

"I told you at dinner you were to discover the truth. Now you know, I'm in training."

He laughed, rose up on an elbow and gazed at her, his emerald eyes sparkling in the dim light. "Sadie, you're not bad. You're the best woman I've ever met. You're someone I'm in awe of. At the moment, I'm exploring where we're going."

"Do you adore me?"

He laughed and she knew he remembered his reference to how he would feel regarding his wife.

"I'm well on my way to adoring you."

"I'm glad," she said and reached up and stroked the side of his face.

She lay relaxing, letting the warm afterglow recede as she stared up at him. This man filled her soul in all the right places. As her papa said, he made her knees grow weak, plus, she thought of him all the time.

"You're definitely not a typical woman. You're a woman I could easily adore."

Why did people assume that a strong woman was an easy woman, when in fact, it was probably the opposite?

A grin spread across her face. Tonight, she'd taken a risk, but after being in his arms, she knew that everything was going to be as it should be. "If you wanted an ordinary woman, then you should never have considered me."

He rolled over, pinning her to the bed. "This has been building between us since that first kiss."

"Earlier. I think it started when you picked me up naked alongside the road."

"You're right," he said, his eyes dark with passion. "Even then, I was attracted to you."

Leaning down, he begin to kiss her neck again, letting his tongue slide along her collar bone, sending tremors through her.

Tonight, she refused to think of what this meant. Tonight, she only wanted to experience pleasure with this man. And she wanted him fiercely. Still did. With him on top of her, his chest against her own, she wanted nothing more than for him to take her again.

Tonight, she hoped, would lead to them being together forever, but for the moment, she only wanted to concentrate on this second. This minute.

Warmth spread through her, and she gazed into Levi's eyes. "Do it again, Levi. Show me again what happens between a man and a woman."

"With pleasure," he said and lowered his mouth to hers.

CHAPTER 25

$\mathcal{E}$arly the next morning, Sadie lay curled around a warm body sleeping soundly. The light was just beginning to awaken her, when she heard a noise in the suite.

"Oh, Levi, darling, sleepy head. We were supposed to have breakfast together this morning," a voice called from the other room.

Her body tensed, bringing her out of slumberland. Oh my goodness, that voice. Her eyes opened just as the door to the bedroom burst wide.

"Lev—" his mother stopped and stared.

Sadie sat straight up in bed, clutching the sheet to her. "Mrs. Griffin."

His mother stood in the doorway, her mouth open, a fierce snarl slowly forming on her face, gathering strength.

"What in hell's name is going on here?" Mrs. Griffin yelled. "Levi, what have you done?"

He had slept with the enemy, that's what he'd done.

"Mother, go away," Levi said, still half asleep. Then, he bolted up in bed as he realized Sadie was beside him.

"You little tramp, you. You are not going to steal my son away.

I don't give a damn how much money you have. He is not marrying a whore."

"Mother, reserve yourself," Levi said. "And get out."

Everything hit Sadie at once. Last night had been a dream, and this morning, the nightmare was beginning. Taking the sheet with her, Sadie rose from the bed, needing to find her clothes and get home. Everyone would be worried about her.

And she didn't want any part of talking to the troublesome Mrs. Griffin who would now make her life a living hell, spreading rumors of her being an easy woman, who she found sleeping in her son's bed.

What had she done?

After Sadie dragged the top sheet with her, she heard a gasp and turned back to see her virgin blood on the sheets.

"You were a virgin?" Mrs. Griffin said, unbelieving.

Humiliation filled her. Of course, the woman wanted to believe the worst about her and here was the proof of her innocence. Betty Griffin would never have believed her pureness, except for the red stain on the sheets.

"Mother, get out. Get out now!" Levi yelled as loud as Sadie had ever heard him. "In fact, get out of my suite."

His mother's face turned red and she put her hands on her hips. "You're choosing her over me? Why is she not leaving?"

"I want her here. Now get out," Levi shouted.

Sadie watched as his mother spun on her heel and marched out, slamming the hotel door behind her.

For a moment, she stood in shock and then panic set in. Now she would truly lose her reputation. Now she would be known as a whore, and yet, part of her didn't care. The night with Levi had been worth every minute.

"I need to leave," Sadie said, glancing around the room for her clothes. They were scattered about, but she could not find her dress. "Everyone will be worried about me. I didn't mean to stay the night."

He wrapped his arms around her. "Take a deep breath. Don't worry. I'll get you home."

That was easy for him to say. He didn't have to worry about his reputation. And his mother would certainly not trash *him* in the paper.

"How can I not be worried? Your mother, the gossip columnist, just caught us together. This is not something I want to read about in the paper. Oh, I'm so ruined."

He ran his hands soothingly down her back. "If she wants me to continue speaking to her, she won't print this in the paper."

"I'm so embarrassed. She saw my blood on your sheets. She knows I was a virgin."

Laughter filled the room. "Stop worrying. She's not going to mention your virgin blood in the paper, that would make *me* the villain and you the *innocent*. It would ruin your evil girl reputation."

Sadie considered that for a moment and then smiled. "You're right, your mother doesn't want me to be seen in a good way. And she will protect you anyway she can. Let's hope she doesn't print this morning."

Being held by him filled her with contentment. They had such a wonderful night together, and now, his mother had spoiled it. All she wanted was to return to his bed, his arms, and yet she knew it was time to leave.

Levi lifted her chin, lowering his mouth to hers. He kissed her gently. "Last night was wonderful. Thank you for making me the luckiest man alive."

She smiled as she stared into his emerald eyes. "You're welcome. Last night was like nothing I've ever known. I'm just sorry we overslept."

He chuckled. "That's because it was almost dawn when exhaustion overtook us."

It was true. They had come together multiple times, each time better and better. The hours had quickly slipped away and then sleep claimed them.

And now this morning, they had paid for their passion with a visit from his mother.

"As much as I'd like to stay, I must get home," she said. "I'm hoping I can somehow slip in. I'm not ready to answer questions about what happened between us last night."

He leaned down and kissed her hard on the mouth and then released her. "Last night was the best night of my life. I can't wait until next I see you."

"I feel the same," she whispered against his mouth. "Don't make me wait too long."

A grin spread across his face. "I won't."

"I'll leave you to dress," he said as he grabbed his pants and pulled them on before he walked into the living area, closing the door behind him.

A few seconds later, he knocked on the door and she opened it for him. "Your dress."

"Oh, thank you," she said and wondered at the reason his mother had continued into the bedroom when her dress had been lying out in the open. The woman had deliberately sabotaged them.

A few minutes later, she opened the door and stepped out. The dress was wrinkled, but still looked nice. But how would she get out of here without someone seeing her?

"My carriage is being brought around and the driver will see you home," he said.

That's what she expected. Levi was a busy man, and this way, hopefully no one would have noticed that she had not come home. She would get the driver to let her out a block away.

"Are you sure you don't want to stay for breakfast?" he asked.

"And share it with your mother?" She gave him a raise brow.

"It could be interesting," he said, both brows raised.

"More likely dangerous to my health," she told him, smiling.

He grabbed her head and brought her lips to his where his mouth ravaged her, letting her know his feelings. When they broke apart, her lips felt swollen, much like the rest of her body.

Oh, how hard it was to leave him this beautiful morning. All she wanted to do was curl up beside him in bed, but that was not possible.

"Have a wonderful day," Levi told her. "If anyone gives you any trouble, inform me immediately."

And she knew he would. He was her defender and she trusted him to make certain his mother did not publish their morning in the paper.

"Good-bye," Sadie said as she stepped out into the hallway. As she walked away, she glanced back at him one last time, hoping that last night was just the first of many pleasant nights with Levi.

The good girl was no longer a virgin. Now she truly did belong to the bad girls' club and what a club it was. No wonder so many women became bad girls. No wonder she wanted to join with him again.

CHAPTER 26

*L*ater that day, Sadie couldn't remember being happier. Flowers had been delivered to the house. Fannie had not said anything when she arrived home, but Sadie knew the woman was not stupid.

She just smiled at her at breakfast and said, "Levi's the one, hmm?"

"Yes," Sadie said, knowing he had not made a commitment to her, but knew that once he felt certain, he would. Last night had been perfect and she was positive she loved him. The quest for a husband was over.

"Well, now I can stay and plan the wedding," she said with a smile.

"Not yet," Sadie told her, wondering how they would ever handle his mother, the writer from hell itself.

They were sitting outside in the shade of the garden. The summer flowers were in full bloom. The bees were enjoying the dahlias and the yellow bells.

"You know, the Cattleman's Ball, the biggest and the last ball of the year, is being held in two weeks."

"Yes, I know," she said, wondering if she and Levi would

attend together? She was trying not to be pushy, letting him take the lead in deciding their future. And if he never proposed, she would be devastated.

She could not even fathom the pain she would feel.

"Ma'am," Julie said, coming to the door. "You have a visitor. A Mrs. Griffin."

"Dear Lord in heaven, what does that biddy want?" Fannie asked. "Maybe I should stay out here and defend you."

At first, she wanted Fannie there beside her, but then she knew Mrs. Griffin might not open up about what she really wanted to talk about if another person were here.

"No, let me speak to her alone. Julie, please bring her out to the garden. Who could be nasty out here?"

"If you need me, don't hesitate to call. I'll be nearby," Fannie said as she went into the house.

Determined to be nice, Sadie stood when Mrs. Griffin walked into the garden. "Mrs. Griffin, it's so good of you to call on me."

The woman looked so angry, she almost appeared evil with the hate spilling from her. Her gray-haired bun was tighter than normal, making her face appear drawn, her dark eyes flashed with fury.

The woman sank down into a chair and glared at Sadie. "This is not a social visit. This is a mother here to protect her son from your conniving ways."

Sadie did not respond. She was not going to let the woman get to her and knew if she said anything it would be taken out of context. This was her beloved's mother, and she would do her best to get along.

She faced Sadie like a warrior preparing for battle.

"Stay away from my son. I don't care that you were a virgin or that he ruined you. I do not want you marrying him."

Disappointment filled Sadie. She dreamed when she married a man, his parents would become her parents, and it was obvious Mrs. Griffin did not want her. And yet she loved Levi with all her heart. Maybe they could come to some kind of agreement or understanding.

"May I ask why you are so against me?"

The woman's face twisted in an ugly snarl. "You're trash."

For a second, Sadie felt a little fear at how the woman seemed like a rabid dog, growling at her.

"What makes me trash?"

"Your father," she said, "years ago, just as I arrived in town, Levi was five years old, you weren't even born yet. Your mother and father had not met. I was looking for work. He refused to hire me. But he tried to make me his mistress."

Even Sadie knew it was possible her father was not as good a man as he'd appeared to be. There were rumors that he kept a woman in the Acre for his pleasure. She realized she didn't know everything about the man who loved her. But this seemed outrageous.

"I'm sorry that happened to you, but how does that make *me* trash. My father was a man who liked to indulge in pleasure. I'd be silly not to recognize that he may have done some ruthless things. But that doesn't mean I'm like him."

The woman frowned at her. "And you think I want grandchildren from your tainted blood? Your father wanted only one thing from me and now my son has gotten my revenge. I'm glad he took your virginity. I'm glad he made you his whore. But I will never let him marry you. The hussy title fits you well."

Was it true that Levi had taken her virginity in order to get revenge for how her father had treated his mother? That didn't seem like something the man she loved would do. This all felt like a lie. A lie to get her to stop seeing him.

"How do I know that this is true?"

"You don't. And I'm telling you that your father tried to make me his mistress. For that reason, I hate your family."

"Well, there's only me, so take out your revenge on me, the only person left, who had no idea this took place."

Mrs. Griffin gave her a smile that was almost evil looking. "Why not? As long as you stay away from my son, it will be our secret."

A trickle of fear went down Sadie's spine. The woman really expected her to give up Levi.

"Mrs. Griffin, I'm sorry my father treated you that way, but you were a strong woman who turned him down. But this happened before I was even born. And if it's true, that Levi took my virginity in order to get revenge for how my father treated you, then he's not the man I want. Your son has been decent and kind to me, quite unlike how you have treated me. Make no mistake, I will talk to Levi about this tonight."

The woman's face grew red. "No. My son does not know the part he played in my revenge."

"There will be no secrets between us," she told the woman.

"Listen to me, little girl," the bitty whisper-hissed, "I will tell of your and A.J.'s illicit night together—" Sadie gasped, wanting to shout it was a lie, but the old woman bulled her way through, "—you know he will back whatever story Nellie pays him to say. And readers will believe all I write as true." She was right. Everyone *wanted* to believe such sensationalism.

"He will recall how you begged him to fuck you out against the saloon building in daylight. How you were completely bare under your dress to be ready for whoever would take you."

Sadie felt sick at such accusations. It would be her word against a popular newspaper columnist, a conniving high-society snob, a man with no morals, and who else?

"My son would be the honest, hardworking, man you lied and tricked into bed even before A.J.'s seed had dried in you."

"But you saw—" Sadie tried to remind her of the broken hymen blood.

"Any woman knows how to prick a finger to make a spot of *virginal* blood. One of the oldest tricks in the book."

Sadie was dumbfounded. How did this woman know so much about such horrible deception?

The woman's vicious hiss continued. "If you are with child, it will be A.J.'s No one will believe anything else."

"No, Levi knows—"

"Levi doesn't know where you are when he works all day in his office. Why, I think I remember someone telling me they saw you at the rail depot at noon, looking for any man who would drop his trousers for you."

"That is a lie—"

"My son is your victim, but he will be redeemed when he marries properly. Just another man duped by a skilled, envious, Jezebel out to steal the only man Miss Robinson, an innocent debutant, has ever loved. Jealous of Miss Robinson's beauty and social status, you set out to her ruination any way possible."

"What?" Was this how Nellie fit into all this? Had this been planned from the start?

"Would you like me to continue on about Fannie's tutelage of you? How she taught you to seduce men, even married men. How she showed you to flaunt your body like Satan himself lived in you?"

The witch's eyes narrowed and a slimy grin stretched across her face. "I am quite the storyteller, Sadie. I will go into detail of how your father lured me into his bed as my infant son was shoved into the arms of saloon whores to care for. How your father promised me love, fortune, everything a woman could want if I would only give up my son who wasn't his—"

Sadie's hand snapped across the face of the woman she now abhorred, ending the false rant. "Don't you dare spread such filth about my father. You can tell the world what you want of me, but I will not tolerate you harming my father's name."

A noise came from the back door. Fannie cleared her throat. "Is everything all right, Sadie?"

What could she say? That she'd just heard the most incredibly horrifying falsehoods she'd ever thought imaginable? A story so hideous, she would be chased out of town for it. "Yes, ma'am. Mrs. Griffin is just leaving."

"You will end your relationship with my son. And you will tell no one of our short meeting here and now, or *else*."

"You want me to break it off with your son, even though we're happy together? That he is in love with me?"

"Yes, it's for his own good. If I tell him, he won't do it, but if you end the relationship, then he'll get over you."

Sadie frowned. How could she marry Levi and get along with his mother after this? Sadie had been willing to forget all the horrible things the mother had done until now.

But she loved Levi. She loved this man. His kindness, his gentle soul, his humor, and how he made her feel like a woman. A beautiful woman who deserved him.

Could she end it with him? She didn't even know if Levi would believe her over so many others.

"I love your son. He's a good man and I think I'm the right woman for him, but I know you're his mother and he loves you. But it wouldn't be fair to put him between us and you're never going to accept me."

The woman smiled. "You're smarter than I thought."

A pain gripped Sadie's chest unlike anything she'd ever felt before. Was this how a broken heart felt? How could they continue with his mother so against them? With this threat looming over them of her putting indescribable lies about Sadie in the paper?

"I'll end my relationship with Levi, not for you, but so that he is not hurt by your lies and deception. But you print one more word about me and I'll go running to him."

"Don't worry, my son is a smart man. He'll get over you."

The woman stood and marched out of the garden into the house. Not saying good-bye. Not even an ounce of politeness in her body.

What a witch.

"How will I ever get over him," Sadie said sitting there.

How could she end her relationship with Levi? She loved him with all her heart and soul and yet his mother would tear them apart. Tonight, she had no choice but to tell him good-bye.

CHAPTER 27

*T*he day seemed to drag by in his office and Levi didn't think it would ever end. He longed to see Sadie. This morning when they were caught by his mother, he didn't have time to speak to his only parent, explain how he realized, today, he was falling in love with Sadie.

He believed the attraction was so strong because their hearts, their souls, seemed to cry out to one another, and he wanted to spend the rest of his life with her. But first, he needed to speak to his mother and calm her before he broached the subject with Sadie.

His mother would not take his decision happily. And it would be tough for a while until she finally accepted and came to love Sadie like he did.

When Levi walked into Sadie's home, he picked her up and swirled her around before he set her down and thoroughly kissed her. When he released her lips, he sighed.

"All day long I've waited for this kiss," he told her. "I couldn't wait to see you again. The apartment seemed so empty after you left."

A smile crossed her face and yet she seemed to be holding

back. It was odd that he knew something bothered her. A sadness seemed to hang about her and he wondered what had changed during the day.

This morning they had both almost been giddy with happiness.

"Come in, we need to talk," she said softly and took him by the hand. Fear spiraled up his spine like a rattlesnake rattling a warning.

"What's wrong? You seem upset," he said.

She led him to the sofa and they sat together. A heaviness seemed to hang over her. The usual giddy, happy woman who didn't let life get to her seemed gone. And he wanted the old Sadie back.

"I've been thinking about last night and your mother walking in on us this morning, and well, I think it's better that I end our relationship."

This was not what he expected. After the night they shared, he truly thought that they would marry. In fact, he'd been thinking about when he would propose, and she was ending what had taken him so long to accept?

This woman had captured his heart and he'd fallen in love for the very first time. This woman was the one he wanted to have a family with, grow old with, and she didn't have those same dreams.

"I'm sorry. I don't understand. We had the best night and today you're ending it? That doesn't make sense to me. When I finally come to the realization that I want to be with you, you decide it's over."

A tear trickled down her face. "We can't be together."

Something dreadful had happened during their separation, because last night and even this morning, they were happy. He knew in his gut they were so very happy.

"Why?"

She reached out and stroked his face, her eyes full of tears. "I'm sorry, Levi. It's for the best."

Anger roared through him unlike anything he'd ever felt before. There had to be a logical explanation.

"Did something happen today while we were separated?"

Could someone have convinced her they were not good for one another? Her new helper? Nellie?

"I've been home all day. Please don't make this any harder. I'm sorry, but it's for the best."

Slowly, he stood. All day long, he'd anticipated being with her, spending time her, talking about their day together while she'd spent the day practicing how to end it with him. None of this made sense and he didn't know how to handle the fact she didn't want him. She didn't love him like he loved her.

He raked his fingers through his hair, shaking his head.

"This was not what I planned on tonight. I thought we'd sit and talk about our day. Kiss, hold each other, and maybe even talk about the future, and I would ask you to go to the Cattleman's Ball with me. Never in my wildest dreams did I think you would end things between us. Especially, when I planned to tell you just how much I'd fallen in love with you."

A gasp came from her and tears rolled down her cheeks. "I'm sorry."

"This is why I never wanted to marry. You've just confirmed my worst fears."

Needing to leave before he said things he would regret, he turned and walked out the door.

When he stepped outside in the summer evening breeze, he took a deep breath as the pain engulfed his heart, shattering the organ into pieces.

Damn. What did he do now? He needed a drink. A stiff drink.

CHAPTER 28

*L*evi went to the White Elephant Saloon where Hayden would be waiting for Mystery Flower to appear. The man was infatuated, and right now, Levi needed to be around people, to drink, and drown his sorrows. To dull the pain that flooded his senses.

Sadie didn't want him. And that hurt worse than any pain he'd ever experienced.

When he walked in the bar, he saw his friend sitting at his usual table with a drink in front of him.

"Levi," he called and then he frowned. "What the tarnation is wrong with you, man?"

"Get me a bottle of something to drink. I don't even care what." Levi had only drank to excess once and the sickness the next morning had been enough to keep him from doing it again. But tonight, he needed something to dull the pain in his chest.

"You look awful," Hayden said. "What happened?"

Hayden motioned for a waitress over. "Bring us a bottle of scotch."

"A bottle?"

"Yes, ma'am. A bottle."

After she returned with the container and two fresh glasses, Hayden poured them each a shot.

Levi immediately slammed one back.

"What's wrong, my friend? You are not a man who consumes liquor like water."

"She broke off our relationship. The first woman I have ever wanted to marry and she ended it tonight."

Hayden didn't respond but poured him another glass. Levi tossed it back, swallowing all at one time.

"We spent last night together. It was magical and I know it was for her as well because the woman came apart over and over in my arms. It was the best night of my life."

Hayden's brows raised, his eyes widening, and he poured himself another glass.

"Did anything happen after last night?"

Levi gave a little laugh and shook his head. "My mother walked in on us this morning. We were entwined together in bed and in she comes. I'm having the hotel change the locks on my doors."

A groan came from Hayden. "I'm sorry, but your mother is hell in a silk dress. Are you certain she didn't have something to do with Sadie changing her mind?"

The man poured him another drink and he swallowed it in a single gulp. Could his mother have gotten to Sadie so quickly?

For a moment, Levi thought about Hayden's comment. He wouldn't have put it past his mother to have spoken to Sadie, but...

"Why wouldn't Sadie tell me that my mother visited her?"

"Maybe she threatened her somehow?"

No, his mother could be daunting, sometimes over the top, but she would never purposefully end his true happiness.

Of course, she would. It was not what *she* wanted. Sadie was not the woman she had chosen for him. And according to her rules, he should only court the women she approved of.

She had caught them and she didn't like Sadie, so maybe he needed to have a discussion with his beloved mother to find out if what Hayden suggested could be true. The woman could have threatened to ruin Sadie's reputation, but she would also have harmed her son, so he didn't think she could stoop so low.

But again, it was his mother. How bad of a story could she concoct and be believable?

"As much as I don't want to believe you, I think I better talk to Mother. The sooner, the better."

Just then the Mystery Flower appeared on stage and Levi knew his friend would be enthralled for the next hour.

"I'm leaving," he said, standing, swaying lightly on his feet, the alcohol going right to his brain. "Enjoy your lady."

"Are you all right? You didn't come here by horse, did you?"

"No, my driver is waiting down the street. I've got to speak to the gossip writer of the newspaper."

He had to know if she had interfered and if she had, there would be hell to pay.

"Be careful," Hayden said. "Let me know how this ends."

"Goodnight, my friend. Thanks for listening," Levi said and walked toward the door. The ground kept moving and he knew he had too much to drink, too fast, with no food. But tonight, and especially right now, he didn't give a damn.

Something to help him forget about Sadie.

Thirty minutes later, he tried to walk without swaying across the hotel lobby to his mother's suite. When he got there, he pounded on the door. It was late, but he had to talk to her now. He had to know if she had ruined his life.

He needed to know the real reason why Sadie had ended their relationship.

"Mother, open up," he cried, pounding on her door again.

Hotel security staff would soon show up and it would not be good to see that he was drunk.

Finally, she opened the door in her nighttime wrapper and ushered him in.

"You've been drinking," she said, astonished.

"You're damn right I have. Tell me, Mother, did you speak to Sadie today? Did you tell her to end our relationship?"

Her back was to him as she lit a lantern and then turned to face him. "What? Of course not. I'm not going anywhere near that little tramp," she said indignant. "I don't even know where she lives."

He loved that tramp. Earlier today, he would have yelled at her for calling her such a terrible name, but now, his pain was so great, he couldn't. As much as he wanted to, it hurt too bad.

"Why do you ask?"

"Because she told me we are over. The first woman I have truly loved and wanted to marry and she ended the relationship."

His mother licked her lips and swallowed. "I'm so sorry, son, but I kept telling you that she was not the right woman for you. Sometimes these things happen for the best."

He sank down onto a chair in her living area. Tears burned behind his eyes. "You never liked her, but I did. She made me realize I did want marriage, a family, and growing old with someone. But it's only with her. Now, I'll never marry."

Just saying the words made him feel even worse. This morning they were happy and tonight it was over. It didn't seem real.

His mother walked over to him and patted him on the back. "Dear, you'll feel that way again. There are plenty of perfect young women available here in town. Soon, you'll be anxious to court someone else. She'll be a distant memory."

Did the woman not understand that Sadie was who he wanted. Looking up at her, he stared. "No. I'm never marrying. Those other women do nothing for me. Sadie was the woman I've fallen in love with. She is the right one for me and now it's over. Sorry, Mother, no grandchildren, no laughing voices, no happiness."

She took a step back, biting her lip and glancing at him. "You truly love her?"

"Yes, I love her sweet smile, the way she always tries to do good even when people were against her. I love to hear her laugh and the way she smells. We were good together, we had fun and now that's gone."

Shaking his head, he stared at her. "You like to interfere. You didn't visit her today and give her some kind of ultimatum?"

"Ultimatum? Really, son, you make me sound like a criminal," his mother said.

"It's just something I fear you would do to get your way," he said.

"I don't always get my way. Tomorrow morning, things will look better. You'll realize there are women even better than Sadie out there."

He stared at her, his head tilting to the side. Why was she always pushing other women on him? "You're certain you didn't talk to her?"

"I think it's time for you to sleep this off," she said, looking away. "Do you need help reaching your suite or do you want to spend the night on my couch?"

Clearly, she was dismissing him. He thought about her reaction for a moment. Why did his mother always seem so cold and focused on getting her way?

Maybe he should ask Fannie whether or not his mother came to speak to Sadie. She would know and he could depend on her to be honest with him. And it was also time to check in with the Pinkerton agent. He wanted to know about his father.

Why did it feel like his mother had secrets she was hiding from him?

CHAPTER 29

*T*he next morning, Sadie didn't get out of bed or go down for breakfast. She had spent the night crying, and frankly, she wasn't ready to be around anyone. Instead, she lay in bed and stared up at the ceiling, wishing she had the bravery to tell Mrs. Griffin to go to hell.

The woman and Nellie had done nothing but cause her trouble and she was tired of them controlling her life. It was over. They had won and she would never have Levi.

None of this seemed fair. She'd been a behaved young lady until two months ago when she accepted Nellie's invitation. Never before had Mrs. Griffin talked about her in the paper, and yet now, she seemed to be their main focus. Why? Because of her attraction to Levi?

A tear trickled down her face and the door to her bedroom suddenly opened. The woman sashayed in like she owned the place.

"Why are you still in bed?" Fannie asked. "Are you sick?"

In a way, she felt ill. Heartsick. Not really wanting to get up and live. Today, she just wanted to feel sorry for herself. After this summer, she deserved the time.

"Last night I ended it with Levi," she said softly. "So, yes, I'm feeling bad."

Fannie sank into a chair near her bed. The beautiful woman gazed at her like she was mad for giving into Mrs Griffins demands.

"Why would you do that? I thought after you were gone all night, you realized you love him?"

Sadie jerked her head toward Fannie. "You knew."

"Yes, I knew. When a woman sneaks in during the early hours of the morning wearing the same dress, her cheeks flushed, and a smile on her face, it's obvious what has happened. And I was so happy for you. But then that dreadful Mrs. Griffin came to visit. What did she do?"

After Mrs. Griffin left yesterday afternoon, Sadie had retreated to her room and not returned until near time for Levi to appear. She'd wanted to hide. Disappear. Look at all the angles and see if there was any way out of appearing in the paper once again that didn't ruin her relationship with Levi.

For the next five minutes, Sadie told her friend and mentor what the woman had said to her. Tears welled up once again when she told her how she had broken it off with Levi to make his mother happy.

"That woman is a bitch," Fannie said. "We are not going to let this woman win. I want you out of bed. We're going to figure out a way to fix this problem."

"But the woman said my father and she—"

"The woman is lying. I don't know why I feel that way, but when does she tell the truth? We'll talk to Eugenia. But I've never heard anything about your father courting another woman. The man never remarried because he loved your mother so much. He grieved for her and never thought another woman could take her place."

Sadie considered this. It was true? She'd often asked her

father why he had never remarried and he said he'd had the best and there was no one else.

"Get dressed. We have much to do."

The woman stood and walked out the door, leaving Sadie. Not even giving her a chance to say she didn't want to get out of bed. One thing was certain, Fannie was not going to let her loiter around feeling sorry for herself. But what could they do?

The breakup had occurred and she doubted Levi would ever forgive her, and how could she tell him that his mother was the one who forced her to end it?

If she married Levi, then Betty Griffin would be her mother-in-law and she would do everything in her power to make their marriage miserable. Could she deal with this woman for the rest of her life?

She would be their children's grandmother. Dear Lord, what could she do?

CHAPTER 30

A week later, Levi walked through the hotel to the restaurant to meet his mother for dinner. It was still hard to pass the room where he and Sadie had dinner. The memory of that night was both a painful and a pleasant reminder. They had such a good time that night and then they had gone to his suite.

Several times, he had rolled over in his big bed searching for the woman he loved only to remember she was no longer here and never would be again.

Then he would lay there the rest of the night, remembering what they had done in his bed, wishing and wanting her.

As he came into the restaurant, he glanced around and saw his mother sitting at the table with Nellie. Dear God, she just wouldn't give up, would she? And the worst part was, she put him in such a precarious position. Nellie's father was the mayor, and right now, he was busy trying to arrange with the city to build a hospital for Fort Worth.

If he made Nellie angry in any way, her father would turn down his proposal. And his business would lose the biggest construction bid they ever attempted with the city.

When he walked up to the table, his mother gave him that wry smile that always got on his nerves. That *I knew I would win* smile.

"Good evening, ladies," he said, knowing his mother had arranged this little dinner date.

"Levi, look who came to have dinner with us tonight," his mother said in that sugary tone that let him know she had arranged this. Soon, they would have another discussion about interference *and* she would find herself alone afterward.

He had reached that point. If she continued to try to find him a wife, he would cut all ties with her.

"Good to see you, Nellie," he replied, thinking how this woman had treated Sadie and as much as he didn't like her, he had to be nice to the woman when all he wanted was to escort her out the door.

"Levi," she said with a smug smile. Oh, yes, this was arranged so that he would forget Sadie. But that would never happen.

He sat at the table, wondering how he was going to handle this situation. Could he be nice to Nellie for one hour without reaching across the table and strangling her?

"Levi, a group of us are going out to the springs tomorrow for a picnic and I was wondering if you would like to join us?"

Oh, the woman had no idea what she had just done. Given him an opening he could not resist.

"I'm sorry, but I'm busy working tomorrow. That is what mature, responsible adults do to make the world a better place. They can't spend time with meaningless, frivolous intentions. Be sure to warn the others about the person who likes to steal people's clothes and leave them stranded."

Her mouth dropped open and her cheeks blushed, and for a moment, he feared she would get up and leave. But he couldn't help but get in a little dig for Sadie's sake.

Then she gave a little giggle. "That sounds intriguing and dangerous."

"It could have been," he said, "leaving a woman naked and

stranded could have had dire consequences, but I came along and picked her up. And to be honest, it was the luckiest day for me. That's the day I met Sadie."

The table was silent and his mother kicked him under the table. The warning signal she had used since he was a kid. But he didn't care. This matchmaking attempt of hers was not going to work. People in hell would get ice water before he ever connected with Nellie.

"The other day I received a thank-you note from Sadie. Very strange. She thanked me for dropping a lemon pie on the two of you. It said the two of you shared the dessert kissing it off each other's lips. To think someone would drop a pie on her at her own ball. Sad."

It was all Levi could do not to spew his food. Sadie had let Nellie know that the pie had brought them together. And he had fond memories of that kiss that night.

"Yes, that lemon pie was delicious. Along with the woman who fed it to me."

Nellie frowned and he knew he had gotten to her. And that's what he wanted. Again, his mother kicked him under the table and he looked at her and smiled.

"Do that one more time, Mother, and you'll be eating alone."

Her eyes grew large, and if he were still a small boy, she would have grabbed him by the arm and yanked him out of the chair. But that wouldn't work today.

The dinner seemed to drag on, and as much as he tried, all he could do was think of the things that Nellie had done to Sadie. Even his mother had never been nice to the woman he loved.

Maybe he should talk to Fannie. He hadn't yet in fear that Fannie would only confirm what Sadie had told him. But she would know the truth regarding why Sadie had ended it with him.

Could his mother have talked to Sadie? She told him no, but

she never approved of Sadie. Why would any of them flat out lie to him?

That morning in bed, they had been so in love. They had not said the words, but the feelings were there. So bright and shiny and new. Then disaster.

Something had happened and before he could walk away completely, he needed to understand what changed.

"Levi, your mother was telling me that you don't have a date for the Cattleman's Ball."

A quick glance at his mother revealed she was smiling happily. Like this was the reason for this dinner and this was what she wanted for her son.

"It's over a week away. There's still time."

"Dear, I think you and Nellie would make a beautiful couple. Ask her to the ball."

Good grief, the woman was bold face telling him what to do? And she had no idea the risk she was putting his new project in. Or did she? She had trapped him exactly like she said she never would.

"I'll take you to the ball," he said almost gritting his teeth. And he would, but that would be the end of it. No more. And his mother would be told to stay completely out of his life. He would find her a new place to live.

His mother patted him on the hand and smiled. "Nellie, you should join us for the hotel's pancake breakfast celebration next Sunday. Our chef prepares the most delicious pancakes with sausage and bacon. The restaurant will have people lined up for hours waiting."

He couldn't help the smile at his thought. "Mother, perhaps *you* should court Nellie. You are taking over and doing an excellent job for me." Was this how his married life would be, his mother always interfering, commanding? Making his decisions for him?

The time for this to end was past due.

162

"Ladies, if you'll excuse me. I have an early day tomorrow and I still need to prep for my meeting."

The meeting was with the city that would determine whether or not he received the permission to build a hospital for Fort Worth. Right now, most doctors' offices had small hospitals in them, but this would be a centralized location where people from anywhere could receive twenty-four care.

"Dear, it's only eight o'clock."

"Sorry, my civil duty calls. It was nice to see you, Nellie. Mother, good night."

He rose from the table and hurried up the stairs. Tomorrow he would learn the fate of the hospital, and then he could tell Nellie that after the Cattleman's Ball they would never see each other again.

And more importantly, he would warn his mother never to demand anything concerning his courting life again.

CHAPTER 31

Mayor Tom Robinson shook Levi's hand. "Congratulations. The city approved the plans you've drawn up for the hospital and we look forward to seeing the building rise in the skyline of Fort Worth."

"Thank you, sir," Levi said, a huge relief filling him. They had agreed to his plans and now he would finalize buying the land and then construction would commence. It was all coming together.

"My daughter, Nellie, told me I'd be crazy not to allow your project," the man said. "And I agreed."

This was the trap he failed to walk away from at dinner last night. His mother's insistence that he take her to the Cattleman's Ball. Not that he had any plans with her afterward. They were done. No longer even friends.

A grimace filled Levi's face. He didn't want to mislead the man. "Tell her I said thank you."

"You can tell her yourself. I hear you're taking her to the Cattleman's Ball."

How did he make the mayor understand that his daughter was not for him?

"Yes, sir. Your daughter is a special young woman. I'll be taking her to the ball, but, sir, I don't think she's the woman for me. This is more of a courtesy event."

The man laughed and that made Levi nervous. Why would he laugh when he told him he wasn't interested in his daughter? The woman had been pursuing him all summer and he didn't like her.

"Son, you're not the only man to tell me that. Her mother and I fret over when she's going to stop being such a little hellion and settle down. But thank you for being honest with me."

Relief filled Levi. "I didn't want you to think the only reason I was taking her to the ball was because of this project. You see, my mother arranged I take her and she doesn't know about the hospital. I don't believe, anyway."

He had kept this project secret for fear it would become a political topic. Some powerful folks didn't want a hospital that cared for everyone. This way, everyone could use it if they chose too.

The mayor smiled at him. "Your mother is kind of like my Nellie. In fact, I'd say they were alike in a lot of ways. And I know, I've been the subject of one of her *About Town* articles."

Strange that the mayor thought that, but he was right. And that was probably why his mother was trying to match him up with Nellie. Someone who had a strong personality like his mother. Another woman to rein him in. Another woman to control him, but he was not having it.

"Strangely, I think you're right. Thank you again, Mayor. I'll see you at the Cattleman's Ball."

The mayor waved and Levi walked out of the courthouse and down Main Street. Since he moved here at the age of five, the town of Fort Worth had grown and changed. They were now trying to clean up the Acre and make it a more respectable area of town. But the cowboys were still coming to visit the saloons and whorehouses, though the cattle drives no longer came through town. At least once a night, there was either a brawl, a gunfight, or knifing in this area of town.

A hospital was needed. The building would help the citizens who lived here and he felt elated at what his little company had accomplished today.

He turned down Rusk and headed to his next appointment. The Pinkerton agent had finally contacted him and said he had a report available. Last night, he'd lain awake wondering if his mother had been honest with him about his father. It was strange that she had yet to produce even one photo of his father. Surely, there had to be one somewhere. A wedding picture perhaps.

When he arrived at the man's office, he entered the building, his boots resounding on the wooden floor.

"Levi Griffin here to see Mr. Wallace."

"Right through that door. He's expecting you," a younger man said.

When he walked in the door, a man stood. "Levi Griffin." Levi put his hand out to shake.

"Jim Wallace," he said. "Have a seat. I have the report ready."

"Thank you," Levi said, wondering if the news was what he wanted to hear or what he feared. Had his mother been honest with him?

"It took our agents awhile to locate the information on your mother and father." The man took a deep breath, and at that moment, Levi realized he was not going to like what he heard. Once again, his mother had lied.

The man was nervous as he began to explain.

"Your mother was raised in Atlanta. Her family was very poor. In 1857, before the Civil War, she was desperate to find a man to marry her. One that was not poor. Your mother was quite the beauty and she fell in love with a Mr. Grant Levison."

Coincidental that he was named Levi? Part of the man's last name. If she was a beauty that would have made it easier for her to join society. But this was right before the war.

Leaning back in his chair, he shook his head. "Mr. Levison was quite wealthy. The first few years together, they were happy. But then the Civil War came and Mr. Levison put his wealth in confederate money. While he went off to war, your mother sold their luxurious home, cashed in her jewelry, and anything of value. When you were four years old, your father died. Not long after, your mother packed up the rest of your belongings and headed to Texas."

The man sighed. "There's only one problem with this story. We can't find a marriage license for your mother and Mr. Levison. We found one for him with another woman, but not for a Betty Griffin. And Griffin is her maiden name, not a married name."

Dumbfounded, Levi sat there staring at the man. So it was true his father was dead, but he never married his mother. And whatever wealth they had, he sacrificed it to the south.

"Any questions?"

"Mr. Levison was married to someone else?"

"Yes, he was," the man said. "In this report is everyone we spoke to. The places we found records, newspaper reports, and even your father's death certificate. As a war widow, your mother would have received money every month from the government, but since she was not married to him, she received nothing."

How had she made money all these years for them to live on? There were so many questions, but maybe she needed to be the one to answer them.

Levi nodded and stood, needing to get back to the hotel and look over the report before he spoke to his mother. "Thank you for finding out and telling me what happened to my father."

"There is a picture of him in the report. I thought you might want to know what he looked like. Also, he is listed as your father on your birth record."

He took the handwritten report from the man, eager to get home and go through it. Why hadn't his mother told him the truth? Why was she hiding that he was illegitimate? Because that would interfere in her quest to marry him off to the most eligible young woman.

If the people of Fort Worth knew he came from an unmarried woman, they would have nothing to do with him. If they knew his mother had a child out of wedlock, they would want nothing to do with her. They would have a society stigma.

While that didn't bother him, he knew his mother would be devastated. She needed to have that association that made her into a big fish in a little pond, while he needed nothing. But Sadie. How would she feel when she learned he was illegitimate?

It seemed like all his mother's life, she'd been searching, striving, to reach the pinnacle of society. What she thought that would achieve, he didn't know. And now he knew the truth and could keep her from ever achieving that milestone.

CHAPTER 32

Sadie walked into the parlor and heard the two women whispering. A week had passed since her break up with Levi and she sometimes felt like she was slogging through mud. Each day didn't seem easier, and at times, she wanted to find Betty Griffin and tell her she'd made a mistake.

But instead, she put one foot in front of the other. Moving forward, but still living in the past.

"Sadie," Fannie said as she walked into the parlor. "Eugenia came to visit."

"Hello, Mrs. Jones," she said and sank onto a horsehair chair that matched the sofa. "Good to see you."

Eugenia reached across the small space and took her hands in hers. "Dear, that witch Betty has been feeding you lies."

For a moment, Sadie was stunned and then she remembered Eugenia had been friends with her mother.

"I knew your mother and father. I watched them fall in love and marry. Betty arrived here right after the Civil War. At that time your father was gone, still in the military. It is not possible for him to know Betty Griffin as she says."

Astonished, Sadie stared at the woman. "I'd forgotten all

about how Papa served in the military during the war. He met mother the month he returned home."

Once again, Mrs. Griffin had lied to gain advantage. But how could she join a family with a woman who hated her so much?

"That's right and they married at the end of that year. There was no time for her to have ever met your father. She's lying," Eugenia said. "She's trying to end your relationship."

How many times had Sadie wished she had stood up to the woman and told her to print that article about her and A.J? Her son would know the truth. That would not happen again.

"And she was successful. I should have been stronger. I should never have agreed to listen to her. But Levi loves his mother and I don't want to come between them. While this is lovely information and makes me feel better that my father was not a rake like she said, she is still Levi's mother."

Eugenia gave a little laugh. "Honey, my sons love me to pieces, but they all believe I'm a big thorn in their sides. But their wives do not put up with me interfering. I've been told politely to step away and let them figure out their own problems. And that's as it should be. But it took interfering for me to learn it the hard way. Betty needs to learn that lesson. And, you, my dear, are going to stand up to her and teach her the same lesson."

Sadie took a deep breath. "I don't know. I fear for me and Levi. It's too late."

The two women looked at each other.

As much as she loved Levi, he loved his mother as much. She had a special place in his heart and maybe it was for the best that she had ended their relationship. But oh, how she missed him. Longed to kiss him, hold him and talk to him softly in bed while they cuddled. There was so much she missed about him.

"You are attending the Cattleman's Ball?" Eugenia asked.

"No, I've changed my mind," Sadie said, knowing she was tired of receiving the ill attention at balls.

"Oh, she will be attending. I'll be right there by her side and Betty will not give us any grief or I'll punch her in the nose."

A smile crossed Sadie's face. Fannie had been a great addition to her life and she was grateful she had the woman here.

Sadie started to giggle. "Fannie, that would certainly make it into her column in the newspaper."

"And it would be worth it," she said with a laugh. "But truthfully, you need to go, to be seen, and look Betty in the eye and call her a liar."

That would be a great opportunity to clear the air.

"You are defending your father's honor," Eugenia said softly.

Her papa didn't deserve to be disgraced this way. She loved him and she would protect his memory. Mrs. Griffin would not dishonor him again.

"Oh, all right. I'll go, but I'm avoiding Levi. But his mother may receive a punch from me. No one lies to me about my papa and gets away with it. No one."

CHAPTER 33

*L*evi worked in his office today. The Cattleman's Ball was tonight and he wanted to spend the afternoon talking to his mother. There was a lot to discuss and he'd not had time until today.

"Mr. Griffin, a Eugenia Burnett-Jones is her to see you," his male secretary said, stepping into his office.

The woman was renowned in the city of Fort Worth. Her sons had cleaned up the town and she played matchmaker for her family and also for other widows in town. Until her own husband, Wyatt, pursued her.

"Bring her in," he said, wondering what she wanted to see him about.

When she came through the door, he stood, walked around his desk and kissed her on both cheeks. "So good to see you. Have a seat. What can I do for you today?"

The woman sat in one of his leather chairs and stared at him. "I'm here with bad news."

For the next hour, she filled him in on why Sadie had broken off their engagement. How his mother had been involved and how she had lied to Sadie about her father.

As he sat there, he didn't know what to do. His mother had done so much damage.

"Son, I doubt you remember when I did matchmaking for my boys. Yes, it worked, but their wives, and even my sons, told me very quickly to stay out of their business or risk being rejected permanently by them. You need to help your mother realize what she's done. It won't be easy. It will not be a pleasant conversation, but she has to realize what she's doing is harmful. The story she said she would write about A.J. and Sadie has not been printed. We consider her to be bluffing. As long as you know the truth to it all."

"How many times have your sons told you?"

She laughed. "At least three times. And the last time, my son, Tucker said stop *or else.*"

"Thank you for coming and telling me."

"Fannie almost came, but I told her it would be better coming from me," she said, rising from her chair. "Now, Sadie will be there tonight. We've convinced her to attend. The rest is up to you."

"Again, thank you, madam," he said as he hurried around the desk and walked her to the door.

Once she was gone, he leaned his head against the door. Damn, but his mother had gotten to Sadie and lied about it.

She didn't realize it, but she was at her last opportunity to change. If such a story was ever printed, it would be the last his mother would ever see of him.

Grabbing his suit coat jacket and his hat, he walked out the office door. It was way past time for him to confront his mother about his father, Nellie, and even Sadie.

He walked into her apartment. "Mother."

"Yes, son," she said, coming out of her bedroom, wearing a fancy dress. "Shouldn't you be getting ready."

"We need to talk," he said, taking her by the hands and leading her to the sofa.

"What's wrong, son?"

"You lied to me," he said softly. "In fact, I've caught you in several lies and I need to understand why."

Her eyes narrowed and she frowned as she shook her head. "Whatever are you talking about?"

Outside her window, the sun was beginning to sink in the western sky, creating an orange glow. He took in a deep breath to calm his raging, furious emotions. "When you never showed me a picture of my father, I hired a Pinkerton man to find out more about him."

Her eyes widened and she gasped. "Whatever for?"

"Because I would have thought there would have been a wedding photo, a picture of him in his military uniform, something that showed me what he looked like. You gave me nothing."

She licked her lips and stared into his eyes. "I told you it's in storage in the hotel attic."

"Mother, do you love me?"

"Of course, son."

"Then don't continue the lie. I know the truth. You see, the Pinkerton man told me there is no marriage license with your name on it. That my father was killed in the war and that the two of you lived together, but that he was married to another woman. I have the report. I have the details of what happened between you. Your maiden name is Griffin."

For a moment, she was silent as she hung her head and sighed. "I loved your father very much, but he was married to a woman he hated. At first, we just saw each other casually, but then it became intense and he wanted to marry me. When I became pregnant with you, he left his wife, and we moved into a house together. Your father was quite wealthy at the time and I was dirt poor."

She sighed. "When the war broke out, of course, he insisted on enlisting and told me we'd wed when he returned. When he said he was going to put his fortune in confederate money, I told him no. That if something happened to him and the money became worthless, I would have nothing. Instead, he put half the money in the confederacy and half he gave to me."

Levi had always known that his mother was a shrewd business woman, but this just proved it even more.

"When I learned that he had been injured, I put the house up for sale. As much as I longed for him to return to me, I knew he never would. The death notice was sent to his wife and she received the widow's pension. You and I were left to fend on our own."

He nodded. "What made you decide to come to Texas?"

"The war would soon be lost and everyone there would always know you as an illegitimate son of Grant Levison. And his wife was making a big hullabaloo of the fact that she was the rightful wife of the dead war hero."

His mother's face looked devastated as she shook her head. "I knew I had to leave the area to give my son a good chance of being a respected member of society. I sold everything, packed up very little, got on a train and we headed out west. The money he split with me is what we've lived on all these years. What helped to start your business. Grant would have been so proud of the man you've become."

With a sigh, he leaned back and gazed at her. "Why couldn't you have been honest with me?"

"Because I didn't want anyone here in Fort Worth to learn the truth about you. That you are illegitimate. That your father was a married man who I loved with all my heart."

Shaking his head, he stared at her. "This is why it's so important that I marry the right girl. To you, it means that you've made it in society."

She closed her eyes and sighed. "When you are raised in a poor home that barely has enough to eat and you know the only reason you got out of that situation was because of your beauty, you want your son to not have to worry about the sins of his

175

parents. You have become wealthy at a young age, but war or a scandal could rob you of that in an instant.

"I would never want you or your children to experience the childhood I had. The hunger. Working hard every day and never seeing any results that could get you out of that hellhole. It was my beauty that attracted your father, and I used my wiles to gain what I needed. A new beginning. But at any moment that could all be taken, leaving you nothing to stand on."

Levi took a deep breath. "So why is Sadie not good enough for me? She's probably the richest heiress in town. She's who I love. Who makes me happy. Why can't you accept her?"

Betty shook her head vigorously. "No. Nellie is the stronger of the women and she's just as wealthy. Sadie's reputation is in shambles and Nellie's father is the mayor. The power is with the Robinson family."

Levi leaned back. "Do you want me to be happy?"

"I want what is best for you and your future."

He sighed as the answer came to him. "Mother, you said my father was married to someone he was not in love with."

"Yes, the woman was vile and manipulative. She was only interested in the things he could give her, in the way he elevated her status among the rich. He was miserable and confided in me how their relationship had become so bad that he considered..." she paused with a sob, "finding a means to end his despair."

"And you brought happiness to him again?"

Her face lit up, tears still trailing her cheeks. "He said I was his reason for living. He'd never felt such joy in his life. His first marriage had been arranged and he never loved her, but what could he do against a powerful father and mother? We loved each other so much, it almost hurt." She laid her hand over her heart.

"Then I had you, and I feared without legitimate standing, we would become destitute and you would spend your life in poverty and any children you had would suffer the same fate. Until you are fully secured in a strong societal position with power and money, I will not stop trying to ensure your success." With that, his mother seemed to wither into herself.

He was stunned from the confession. Never had he expected his mother to have such a heart-wrenching past. Lord, so many questions about their lives, he now had answers to. The motivation for her unrelentless drive for only the best for him. The reason behind all her choices for them, including his future wife.

Yes, now he understood why his mother had chosen Nellie. Money wasn't enough of a safety net. She'd experienced how easily wealth could disappear. Nellie's father as mayor could blaze a path for him into any area of business he desired, giving safety and security.

Had she not seen that he had made and secured his own future? He was well diversified in many financial aspects. Construction, railroads, hotels. She had taught him well in money management. Perhaps it was time for him to return the favor.

He took her hands into his. "Mother, there are so many thoughts we need to share based on this revelation, but now, I need you to imagine what I'm about to explain to you. Can you do this for me?" She nodded. "Let's pretend that I am my father when he was in his prime. Nellie is Father's unloving wife. And you are...Sadie."

His mother drew in a sharp breath as she stared into his eyes. Funny how life repeated itself through generations if not careful. He saw her mentally making the connections he had with old and new, and after a moment, she burst into tears.

"Oh my Lord," she cried, "I had no idea...I didn't see...I-I—"

He gathered her into his arms as she sobbed. Of course, she hadn't seen the consequences of her well-intended mechanizations. Her focus was on making sure he would be happy and she thought she knew how to make that happen for him. But only he could be the decider of that.

"I am so sorry," she said sniffling. He pulled out his handkerchief for her. "See, you are the perfect gentleman. I want so much for you. Everything I didn't have. That's what parents want for all their children. I meant no harm—" She burst into another ball of tears.

He pulled her in and kissed her forehead. "I know, Mother. I've always felt your love for me. And I hope you have felt mine in return."

She nodded. "I do."

"Since the time for the ball grows near, may I make a suggestion on how I would like to see the event happen tonight?"

"Of course," she dabbed at her nose like a seasoned lady.

"Today, I learned you told Sadie lies in order to keep us apart." His anger and bitterness had fled with the light of banished secrets. He was ready to begin the healing process. "If you want to be in my life and those of my family, you need to apologize to her. You will do your best to get along, because I intend on asking her to be my wife, if she will accept me. Sadie is my reason for living. She brings me joy like I've never felt with anyone."

"I understand now," she replied.

"I will not accept your interference again. If you want to be in your grandchildren's lives, you will accept Sadie and not interfere again."

Tears filled her eyes. "Yes, son, I understand."

He stood, lifting his mother to her feet with him. "We should be going if we are to arrive on time. Or would you prefer the three of us to make a grand entrance?"

CHAPTER 34

Sadie stood next to Fannie. "Oh, how I wish I had not let you talk me into attending this sorry ball."

"The night is young," Fannie said. "Smile and try to have a good time."

How could she when she'd seen Levi and Nellie arrive together with his mother? Then Nellie had given him a hug and departed from his side. Odd that she had walked away from her escort. But who was she to concern herself any longer with Nellie and Levi's affair? May they have a loving marriage and future.

Tears sprang to her eyes as her heart caved in despair. "I'll return shortly," Sadie said as an excuse to meander through the crowd of people, say hello to Rose and Tessa, if she could find them.

When she passed A.J., he gave her a smug smile and she shuddered with revulsion. The man was despicable and she wouldn't wish him onto any woman.

Tessa came up to her. "Dear Moses, have you heard?"

"No, what?"

"Rose's father has found her a man to marry. He told her he expects her to marry within the week."

"Oh no, is she here?"

Tessa shook her blonde hair. "No, I haven't seen her. I'm worried about her."

"Me too," Sadie said. "If you see her, tell her she is welcome to move in with me."

A smile spread across her friend's face. "Don't tempt me or I'll move in with you as well. We could make it the Bad Girls' Club. They told me I can't compete in the national shooter's contest. I know it's because I'm the best and they're afraid of me. But they're telling me it's because I'm a woman."

Sadie smiled. "Then become a man."

"What do you mean?" Tessa said, staring at her.

"Put on some trousers, a shirt and hat, and make yourself look like a man. And then go and beat them at their own game."

A smile crossed Tessa's face as she realized how to solve the problem.

"No wonder you're called bad. You're wonderful. All I need is a name, some clothes, and practicing a male voice, and they'll never know. Thank you, my friend."

Impulsively, Sadie reached out and hugged her. "I love the idea of the Bad Girls' Club. Fannie is there to chaperone us, and well, I'm not going to let society rules get to me any longer. I'm going to live my life to the fullest."

"That's right," Tessa said. "And I'm going to join you. Now we just need to find Rose and learn what she's up to. I'm going in search of her."

Sadie nodded as she glanced around the ball room. "I'll do the same."

They parted, each going a different direction as Sadie continued to work her way through the throng of people to a more private room. When she pushed open the door, Nellie was inside.

"Sadie, we meet once again."

"Yes, we do," Sadie said, biting her lip. Of all the women to run into. "I hope you're happy. Looks like you won. I hope you and Levi will be very happy together."

In a green evening gown that made her look stunning, the woman turned and stared at her. What a shame they could never be friends.

Nellie started to laugh. "We've had our differences. I hope you realize that the only reason I mistreated you was because I was jealous of you."

The woman tossed her blonde hair like she was the queen.

"That's sad, because I wanted to be your friend."

"Sorry, that's not going to be. I'm never friends with anyone who is prettier than I am. But I won't be bothering you anymore. I've been told that if I harm, embarrass, or harangue you in anyway, there will be dire consequences."

Sadie wondered who had told her to leave her alone.

"Well, now that you have Levi, there's no need."

Nellie smiled and walked out the door.

An overwhelming sadness came over Sadie. Everything seemed lost. As she walked down the stairs to the ballroom, Mrs. Griffin came to her. "May I have a word with you, Sadie?"

Well, damnation. What was it, confession of the soul night? It was all she could do not to say no. "I have done as you asked, and then I realized my father was in the military. There was no way he could have met you. You lied to me."

At least she spoke up to the woman and defended her father's honor.

Mrs. Griffin took her by the arm and led her outside. A sense of fear overwhelmed Sadie. Once before, she'd been tricked in the garden. This time, she was prepared as she doubled her fists. Ready to fight.

A quick glance confirmed they were alone, but still she would not be taken by surprise.

"I want to apologize," Mrs. Griffin said, her chin dropping to her chest.

Sadie froze and stared at her as disbelief overwhelmed her. "Pardon, what?"

"I'm sorry I impeded on your life. A mother only wants what's best for her son and sometimes we're clouded by our own wants and desires. I'm sorry I came between you and Levi. I promise you, it will never happen again."

Sadie narrowed her eyes at the woman. "You're not going to write horrible things about me or my father or anyone I love in the paper again?"

The woman smiled at her. "No, dear. I won't. Now as I think back, I am truly ashamed of what I threatened. My anger at my own failures fueled my fury which I released on you. I would never print such horrible words, even if the story were true. When you have your own children, you will understand from my view, but still, my threats are inexcusable. Will you please accept my apology?"

"I'm just surprised. First Nellie, and now you." She glanced up at the sky. "Is the moon full?"

Why did this all seem so weird?

"No. I've been shown the error of my ways and I have promised I will be a better mother and person. Now, I think we should return and enjoy the ball."

Still in a state of shock, she let the woman lead her back inside.

As they walked through the door, Levi stood there. Not giving her a chance to respond, he took her arm. Astonished, she stared up at him.

"What is happening?" she asked. She felt like a hot potato passed around the room.

He only smiled.

"Thank you, Mother," he said and led Sadie onto the ballroom dance floor.

The crowd parted. What was going on? Why had the music stopped and all eyes were on the two of them?

"What are you doing," she hissed. If this was to be a reveal of his mother's horrendous made-up story, she was going to bust noses as Fannie suggested.

He grinned at her. "Just wait."

When they reached the center of the room, he dropped to one knee and her mouth fell open.

"Sadie King, on the day we first met, you grabbed my attention. After I made my decision to never to marry, you made me realize the fun, the laughter, the warm moments I was missing. We've had some rocky periods, but I've believed in you. But most of all, I've fallen in love with you, and you're the only one I want to share my life with. Will you marry me and spend the rest of my life by my side, letting me adore you?"

Tears sprang to her eyes, and suddenly, she knew that he had learned the truth about how his mother had deceived her. That's why his mother apologized.

"Can you love a bad girl?"

"Bad girls are the best," he said with a wink. "And you're not a bad girl. You're the most amazing woman I've ever met. You're my girl."

A smile spread across her face. "But I thought, you and N—"

"You were wrong," he said. "Will you marry me?"

"Yes, oh, yes," she said and pulled him up. Their lips came together and he kissed her like he wouldn't let her go. Finally, she pulled back. "Oh, Levi. I love you so much. I've been miserable these last couple weeks."

He smiled down at her. "When I learned the truth, I made certain my mother knew not to ever obstruct again. But I don't think she has plans for that either now."

"I didn't want to come between the two of you," she said. "She's your mother."

"And you won't. You are to be my wife and you are who I will always trust and listen to."

People started to offer their congratulations. Finally, Mrs. Griffin came up to them carrying three glasses of champagne. She handed each of them a glass.

"A toast, to my future daughter. May you and my son have a wonderful life together filled with love and laughter."

"Thank you," Sadie said.

His mother looked at each of them. "You're right, son, I see she makes you happy. You are wise to choose her."

"Thank you, Mother," Levi said as they clinked their glasses together.

The music began to play once again and Levi handed the empty glasses to his mother. "Will you dance with me, Sadie?"

"I'd love to dance with you for the rest of my life."

"Scandalous Sadie, I adore you."

* * *

THE FIRST BOOK in the series is often the hardest one to write, because you don't know how the series is going to work. And yet, I loved Levi, even with his cantankerous mother. Who will also show up in the next book and book four. Want a sneak peak at Ravenous Rose? Keep reading...

* * *

Ravenous Rose

ROSE TUTTLE, the preacher's daughter, ran through the darkened streets of Fort Worth toward Hell's Half Acre. Fear filled her as she hurried down the back alleys, knife in hand.

Clenching the weapon in her fingers, she knew that no one would stand a chance against her at the moment.

Tonight, she had been planning to attend the Cattleman's Ball with her parents, but then her father introduced her husband-to-be to her.

A gangly, ugly man who was a preacher in a small town three hours west of Fort Worth. A man who looked at her with such lecherous desire in his eyes that he frightened her. Chilling was the only way to describe the carnal glee radiating from him.

Even the men in the saloon didn't gaze at her that way. They looked at her with adoring eyes, but this man glowered at her, like he couldn't wait to strip her down and do evil things to her body.

When she voiced her objections, her father had taken her aside and told her she would marry this man tomorrow. That her time of searching for a godly man was over. He had found her one. Her rebellion was at an end.

All she could think was that she had to get away. She excused herself, snuck into another room, opened a window, and crawled out.

Now she was escaping to the White Elephant Saloon, her safe haven. The place where she could pretend her life was not the disastrous mess she hated. Her one escape.

Reaching the back of the saloon, she pulled open the door and entered. The stage manager glanced at her.

"I thought you were going to the Cattleman's Ball tonight," Randal said. He was the only one who knew who she really was and approved of her disguise.

"No, I'm not going to the ball. Where's my costume?"

"Are you all right?"

"No, I'm terrified. My father has found me a groom. We are to be wed tomorrow."

The man's eyes widened and he handed her the outfit she normally wore. A demure dress for a woman in a saloon with lace ruffles at the bottom and a low cut bodice that she had added more lace to hide the swells of her breasts. She went into the curtained off area and quickly changed.

"I'm not marrying him. He terrifies me." Her shoulders hunched as a shiver ripped through her body.

"Calm down, Rose. Take a deep breath. We'll figure something out."

"He's a preacher. I don't want to be a preacher's wife. I've seen how my father's congregation treats my mother and I will not be subjugated by my husband or his people."

She tossed her dress aside and pinned her tiny reticule inside her stage outfit. It contained all her cash and she feared she was going to need that money in the coming days—everything she'd earned the months of singing here.

The many months of sneaking out to do what she loved.

When she stepped out, he helped her with her hat and the thick veil that covered her face. She could barely see through the tightly woven lace.

"Are you ready?"

Taking a deep breath, she grinned at him. "I'm ready. This is what I love. This is where I belong."

As soon as she said the words, it hit her. All she had to do was rip the veil off and let the men see who she was. That would ruin her. She would no longer be a woman a preacher would want to marry.

She would be a bad girl.

It seemed the perfect solution, but could she do it? What if the audience only loved her because of her mysteriousness?

Then not only would she be ruined, but she'd have no way to make a living.

Randal led her up the stairs to the stage and then he left her waiting in the shadows. The piano player was banging out music, which abruptly came to a halt.

"Ladies and gentlemen, we have a special surprise tonight.

Mystery Flower was not supposed to appear, but she's here and she can't wait to sing for you. Please welcome, Mystery Flower."

An energy that excited Rose every time she sang spiraled through her when she came out on stage.

"Good evening," she said, excitement filling her. "Tonight, I was supposed to attend the Cattleman's Ball, but who wants to be with a crowd of boring socialites? Instead, I decided to be with you."

The crowd went wild with cheering and clapping.

Then she saw him sitting at his usual table, a drink in his hand as he stared at her. There was something about the man that always gave her a little thrill. Just staring into his eyes, a warmth would overcome her.

For months, he had attended her shows, sitting in the back, never approaching her. Always watching.

Her breath seemed to catch in her throat and she leaned her head back and began to belt out a song that she loved. The men raised their drinks in the air, cheering for her.

This was where she belonged. This was what she wanted to do. Sing. And her voice was a gift from God, to bring the people joy.

As the night wore on, she belted out song after song, the audience yelling, clapping and even singing along.

On the last song of the night, she began a ballad that everyone knew. The men, most of them quite drunk, sang along with her. And when she reached up and began to unwrap her disguise, they all stopped and stared.

Piece by piece, she removed the veil and finally the hat. She stood in front of them, holding out the last note of the ballad in her natural glory. Her face revealed.

The preacher's daughter had been exposed. No longer would she be anonymous.

When she finished, they all clapped and stomped their feet and a few even fired their guns off at the ceiling.

"Rose, Rose, Rose," they screamed.

"Good night, gentlemen," she called.

After she walked off the stage, she went back to the dressing room and changed her clothes. It was over, she was ruined. She wasn't even sure they would allow her to sing in the saloon again.

Now, the preacher man would no longer want her, but what would she do?

When she walked out of her dressing room, the man who sat at the table watching her every night was waiting.

His hands reached for her face and he pulled her to him and she watched in awe as his lips came crashing down on hers. Rose had never been kissed before and the way his mouth seemed to control hers, she didn't know what to think except that a heat begin to build inside her and she didn't want him to stop.

She didn't even know his name. Her hands came up between them and she pushed him away. The most sparkling blue eyes gazed at her and she wanted to lose herself in them. Sandy brown hair came to a peak on his forehead with his hair combed straight back. A straight nose, narrow jaw, small lips with dimples in his chin made her smile. But most of all...that kiss.

"What are you doing?"

"Rose Tuttle," he said, ignoring her question. "For months, I've wanted to kiss you."

"You shouldn't be back here," she answered.

"I gave the bouncer a gold coin. May I escort you home?"

That was such a tempting offer. It was a long walk to Sadie's home. She risked her father finding and taking her back to marry that horrible man. Maybe she should accept his kind offer.

"No, but you may accompany me to my friend's house, Sadie King. You see, I'm not returning home ever again."

He gazed at her steadily. "When you removed your disguise and the men told me who you were, I knew there had to be more to this story. Allow me to take you to your friend's home, and on the way, you can tell me what happened."

There was something about this man that made her think she should know him. But she didn't. And yet, he watched her every night for months. Applauded her, cheered her, and she felt a connection to him.

"I'm sorry, but I don't know your name," she said.

He bowed his head to her. "Hayden Lee. I have a business proposition to discuss with you."

She frowned at him. What could the man want with her? "And what would that be?"

"I'd like for you to become my mistress."

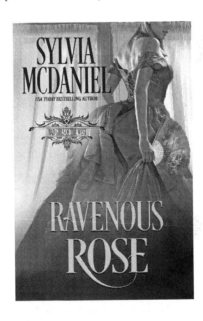

PLEASE LEAVE A REVIEW

Did you enjoy the book? Reviews help authors. I would appreciate you posting a review.

Follow Sylvia McDaniel on Facebook.
http://facebook.com/SylviaMcDanielAuthor

Sign up for my New Book Alert at www.SylviaMcDaniel.com and receive a complimentary book.

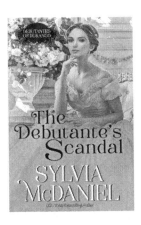

The Debutante's Scandal

SYLVIA McDANIEL

Meg Trippe and her sisters, Fannie and Daisy, walked around the dress shop gazing at the newest fabrics and the latest fashion the small town of Durango, Colorado, had acquired.

"Look at this yellow silk. Wouldn't that make a beautiful dress?" Daisy said.

"Do you think Papa would let you buy that? Ha!" Fannie said.

"Probably not, but Mama would. When she comes back from her tea, I'm going to ask her."

Meg shook her head. "Just put it on the bill. Mother will give you anything you want. You are the favored one."

Meg's fingers trailed across the bolts of material. Oh, how she loved creating her own designs from fabric. The very reason she wanted to go to New York City and learn how to professionally design the latest fashions.

Even her mother admitted she was quite the dressmaker, stitching her own clothes, cutting out a pattern, making small changes that gave the design her own special flare.

As soon as the weather warmed, she would be leaving to attend Miss Johnson's Design School in New York City and she could hardly wait.

Fannie lifted a purple taffeta material. "What do you think?"

"I think with your auburn hair, you would be the belle of the ball," Meg said.

"Not if I'm there," Daisy replied.

Fannie stuck her tongue out at her. "Brat. It's all about you."

Daisy laughed and tossed her blonde hair to the side. "Why not? As you and Meg like to say, I am the favored one."

"Let's all pick out a fabric and Meg can make us a dress. That way we'll have it for the debutante ball," Fannie said.

"But I can't attend this year. Not for two years," Daisy whined.

"It's because you're a baby," Fannie said.

Oh, how Fannie loved to antagonize Daisy, but usually her baby sister gave back as good as she received. Sometimes even better.

"Ladies, I hear rumors that there is going to be a special visitor at the ball this year," the dressmaker Madam Juliette called out. "Meg, I have some new catalogs you might be interested in checking out. Some gorgeous new fashions."

Meg didn't care about meeting a special visitor or finding a husband. She had plans. Plans that didn't include a man. But this would be an opportunity to showcase her designs.

Papa was wealthy enough he could afford for them all to have a new dress.

"Thank you, Madam Juliette."

Tonight, she would spend time devouring the latest fashions. Then she would sit with her sisters and create the perfect gown for the ball.

Carrying a bolt of peach satin to the counter, she also took a small bolt of the same color of organza. With her dressmaking skills, she would create beautiful party dresses for everyone, but Daisy.

She would have to wait.

Also By Sylvia McDaniel
Western Historicals
A Hero's Heart
Second Chance Cowboy
Ethan

American Brides
**Katie: Bride of Virginia

Angel Creek Christmas Brides
**Charity
**Ginger
**Minne
**Cora

Bad Girls of the West
Scandalous Sadie
Ravenous Rose
Tempting Tessa
Nellie's Redemption

The Burnett Brides Series
The Rancher Takes A Bride
The Outlaw Takes A Bride
The Marshal Takes A Bride
The Christmas Bride
Boxed Set

Lipstick and Lead Series
Desperate
Deadly
Dangerous

Daring
**Determined
Deceived
Defiant
Devious
Lipstick and Lead Box Set Books 1-4
Lipstick and Lead Box Set Books 5-9
Lipstick and Lead Box Set Books 1-9
**Quinlan's Quest

Mail Order Bride Tales
**A Brother's Betrayal
**Pearl
**Ace's Bride

Scandalous Suffragettes of the West
**Abigail
Bella
Mistletoe Scandal

Southern Historical Romance
A Scarlet Bride

The Cuvier Women
Wronged
Betrayed
Beguiled
Boxed Set

The Debutante's of Durango
The Debutante's Scandal
The Debutante's Gamble
The Debutante's Revenge
The Debutante's Santa

** Denotes a sweet book.

Want to learn about my new releases before anyone else? Sign up for my New Book Alert and receive a complimentary book.

USA Today Best-selling author, Sylvia McDaniel obviously has too much time on her hands. With over fifty western historical and contemporary romance novels, she spends most days torturing her characters. Bad boys deserve punishment and even good girls get into trouble. Always looking for the next plot twist, she's known for her sweet, funny, family-oriented romances.

Married to her best friend for over twenty-five years, they recently moved to the state of Colorado where they like to hike, and enjoy the beauty of the forest behind their home with their spoiled dachshund Zeus. (He has his own column in her newsletter.)

Their grown son, still lives in Texas. An avid football watcher, she loves the Broncos and the Cowboys, especially when they're winning.

www.SylviaMcDaniel.com
Sylvia@SylviaMcDaniel.com
The End!